He spoke with a **staff scrambli** **who _wouldn't_ asked if it mea** **killer smiles?**

His long eyelashes were partly to blame for his appeal to women, she decided. Add dark brown hair and blue eyes, a firm jaw and an attractive dimple, and infatuation was a given.

While he wore the requisite surgical green scrub suit under a protective yellow paper gown, the shapeless garments didn't detract from his muscular shoulders or his lean physique. If he could turn heads in this ugly garb, he'd probably stop traffic when he wore street clothes that actually fit. If the hospital ever created a doctor-of-the-month calendar featuring him as the centerfold they'd make a fortune.

As great as his physical appearance was, he wouldn't have earned the moniker of "the delectable Dr. Donovan" if he didn't have the personality to match. His charisma explained how he'd managed to get whatever—and whomever—he wanted in his department. His persistence and eloquent arguments had persuaded several top people to transfer her into his domain.

Apparently aware of her lingering presence, he flashed her a cocky grin.

Hating that he'd caught her loitering, and was obviously thinking she'd become one more member of his adoring fan club, she fled the room.

Dear Reader

One day I stumbled across an article about labyrinths and their associated healing effects. I was intrigued by how hospitals in the US are building these labyrinths on their campuses to help patients achieve spiritual health while their medical needs are addressed. I began my research and was fascinated by what I learned.

Consequently, I wanted to incorporate this concept into a story. I've taken a few liberties for my own purposes, but I simply had to create characters who needed the emotionally healing effects of a labyrinth.

I hope you enjoy what I've done. Happy reading!

Sincerely

Jessica Matthews

MAVERICK IN THE ER

BY
JESSICA MATTHEWS

MILLS & BOON®

First published in Great Britain 2011
by Mills & Boon, an imprint of Harlequin (UK) Limited,
Eton House, 18-24 Paradise Road, Richmond, Surrey TW9 1SR

© Jessica Matthews 2011

ISBN: 978 0 263 88591 0

Harlequin (UK) policy is to use papers that are natural, renewable and recyclable products and made from wood grown in sustainable forests. The logging and manufacturing process conform to the legal environmental regulations of the country of origin.

Printed and bound in Spain
by Blackprint CPI, Barcelona

Jessica Matthews's interest in medicine began at a young age, and she nourished it with medical stories and hospital-based television programmes. After a stint as a teenage candy-striper, she pursued a career as a clinical laboratory scientist. When not writing or on duty, she fills her day with countless family and school-related activities. Jessica lives in the central United States, with her husband, daughter and son.

Recent titles by the same author:

EMERGENCY: PARENTS NEEDED
HIS BABY BOMBSHELL
THE BABY DOCTOR'S BRIDE

To Terry, for being my hero.

CHAPTER ONE

LET this be a lesson to you, Sierra McAllaster, she told herself in her rush to meet the incoming ambulance. *Never say never.*

She'd worked in Emergency Services before coming to Pennsylvania three months ago, and when she'd left North Carolina, she'd vowed that daily E.R. duty wouldn't be in her future. She'd been there, done that, and although she'd once loved her work in that hectic department, it was time to pass the torch to others who thrived on the adrenalin rush. She wanted a more sedate pace with patients who weren't broken bodies in need of an immediate fix, and she'd found it on the fifth-floor medical unit at Pittsburgh's Good Shepherd Hospital.

However, just when she'd finally settled in to her new duties, her career plan had taken a one-hundred-and-eighty-degree turn. At this very moment she was in the middle of the very position she'd never intended to fill again, thanks to a one-sentence clause in the fine print of her contract.

"Come on, people," Trey Donovan, the senior emergency physician, yelled beside her. "Let's move!"

By the time their small entourage had reached the ambulance bay, two paramedics were already tugging a stretcher out of the back of their vehicle.

A feeling of dread swamped her, but she reasoned it away. *You don't know this person. None of your friends or family could possibly be on that stretcher. This is a car accident—nothing at all like David's situation.*

She swallowed hard and forced herself to fall back into her objective professional mode.

"MVA," one medic reported, using the shorthand Sierra recalled so vividly. *Motor-vehicle accident.* "Forty-five-year-old male with blunt trauma to the chest and abdomen, dislocated shoulder and sundry other injuries. BP is…"

Sierra noted the vital signs as she gazed down at the man lying on the gurney, strapped to a backboard and wearing a cervical collar. Bruises were already forming on his visible extremities and lacerations from broken glass crisscrossed his face. An oxygen mask covered his nose and mouth, but his nose was swollen and clearly broken, which meant they'd need an airway.

"Let's go," Trey ordered, and off they scurried to the nearest available trauma room.

"He's wearing a MedicAlert bracelet," the other paramedic reported. "According to the company records, he's a diabetic and he's currently taking Coumadin, hydrochlorothiazide and something called liraglutide."

The blood-pressure medicine wasn't unusual for someone his age, but the blood thinner was. "Has he had a recent heart attack or stroke?"

"We don't know, but his left knee has a freshly healing scar. Maybe a recent joint replacement? The police are trying to locate his next of kin."

"Any record of insulin?"

The paramedic shook his head. "None."

"What was that last drug you'd mentioned?" Trey asked, his brow furrowed as if trying to place the medication.

"Liraglutide," the paramedic repeated.

Trey turned to one of the nurses. "Call the Pharmacy and ask—"

"Don't bother," Sierra interrupted. "It's a new drug just approved by the FDA for treating type 2 Diabetes."

"Oh."

Trey's dark-eyed gaze met hers over the gurney and she read his unasked question. "I had a patient who had trouble controlling his diabetes, so we tried it. It's not the first line of therapy and has a number of side effects, but in his case it was a last-ditch resort and it worked," she explained.

He grinned, and the most endearing dimple appeared in the side of his cheek. "Your first official day and you're already handy to have around."

Strangely enough, her face warmed under his appreciative comment. Sierra McAllaster did *not* respond to empty flattery with a blush, she reminded herself. Thanks to her husband, who'd liberally used his charm to his own advantage, she'd eventually determined it was merely a tool to get what he wanted. The lesson had been painful to learn as her illusions had been shattered, but she'd never forget it. Never again would she fall for a fellow who troweled on charm as easily as a brickmason laid his cement. She'd become immune to men like him.

However, immunized or not, it seemed rude to refuse to return his smile so she did, even though she didn't know why she was smiling in the first place.

A few seconds later, they'd pushed the gurney against the awaiting bed in the trauma room. Sierra locked the wheels in place with the toe of one pump, having already decided she'd overdressed for the demands of this department. She'd forgotten the frantic pace—or maybe she'd simply blocked it out of her mind—which meant a dress and heels weren't her most practical choice of attire.

"Lift on three," Trey ordered. "One, two, three."

Everyone complied in one smooth, well-rehearsed motion to move their patient to his new bed. Sierra hoped any residual blush on her face could be attributed to the strain and not Trey's flattering comment.

"Can you hear me, Mr. Klein?" Trey spoke to the fellow. "You're in the hospital and we're going to take care of you."

Unable to nod because his head and neck were immobilized, he simply blinked and mouthed, "Okay."

Sierra hung around and helped the nurses organize the patient's tubes and swap the paramedics' equipment for hospital-issue while Trey issued orders for X-rays and lab work, requesting the same procedures Sierra would have if she'd been in charge of this case.

His next command caught her by surprise. "Go to lunch, Sierra."

She paused. "You don't need help?"

He shook his head and flashed his trademark grin. "Thanks, but I'm good."

Yes, he was, she thought as she moved out of the way, somewhat reluctant to leave just yet. Instead, she took a few minutes to observe her colleague in action.

Today might be her first official day in Emergency, but it wasn't the first day she'd worked with Trey. In her previous position as hospitalist on the fifth-floor medical unit, she'd received several patients he'd admitted and had answered his call for a consultant on numerous occasions. His medical skills then, like now, seemed outstanding.

He spoke with a calm authority that sent staff scrambling to obey, but she could tell they did so out of a desire to please rather than a sense of fear. Then again, who wouldn't want to do whatever he asked if it meant receiving one of his killer smiles? She'd seen how his grin had turned even the most independent, career-minded woman into the equivalent of a simpering teenager.

He was also more than just a handsomely wolfish smile. His long eyelashes were partly to blame for his appeal to women, she decided. Add dark brown hair and midnight-blue eyes, a firm jaw and an attractive dimple, and infatuation was a given.

He was a tall man, which made nearly every female, no matter her size, feel dainty and feminine. While he wore the requisite surgical green scrub suit under the protective yellow paper gown, the shapeless garments didn't detract from his muscular shoulders or his lean physique. If he could turn heads in this ugly garb, he'd probably stop traffic when he wore street clothes that actually fit.

If the hospital ever created a doctor-of-the-month calendar featuring him as the centerfold, they'd make a fortune.

As great as his physical appearance was, he wouldn't have earned the moniker of "the delectable Dr. Donovan" if he didn't have the personality to match. His charisma explained how he'd managed to get whatever—and whomever—he wanted in his department. Because of his persistence and eloquent arguments that she was the one physician who could immediately fill the long-vacant position in his service, he'd persuaded several top people to transfer her into his domain. Granted, she was only covering until the heads of Emergency Services and Internal Medicine hired a physician specifically for the post but, as far as she was concerned, a day spent in the ED was one day too many.

Apparently aware of her lingering presence, he flashed her a cocky grin.

Hating that he'd caught her loitering and was obviously thinking she'd become one more member of his adoring fan club, she fled the room. After a brief stop at the staffing board, where she slapped a Lunch magnet beside her name, she hurried outside, into the warm afternoon sun.

Trey surreptitiously watched Sierra leave as if a rabid dog were nipping at her heels and hid his smile. He'd first met her three months ago when he'd called the fifth-floor medical unit to request a stat internal medicine consult and Sierra had responded, barely giving him a second glance.

Accustomed to dealing with flirty and simpering females, Trey had been taken aback by her disinterest at first but then he'd been intrigued by it. In his earlier life as a footloose, carefree bachelor, he would have responded to the challenge she presented and pursued her with everything he had. However, that had all changed when his sister-in-law, Marcy, had died. While his relationships were still of the short-term variety, he'd come to the conclusion that even those were difficult to juggle with everything else in his life. Acting as Mitch's "big brother," helping Mitch raise his niece and coping with the demands of his job took nearly all of his free time.

As much as he'd like to know Sierra on a more personal level, his gut told him that she wasn't the sort who would embrace such a temporary and superficial relationship.

Instead, she was the type to make a man think about the future in terms of the next twenty or thirty years. At times, he tried looking ahead that far, but he simply wasn't ready to let a woman get that close. Between coping with Mitch's downward spiral after Marcy's death and his struggle to meet all of his family obligations, he didn't have the time or the energy to devote to anyone else.

That hard truth, however, didn't prevent him from wishing Sierra would be happy with what he could offer, especially after today when he'd seen her face turn a beautiful shade of pink. What woman in this day and age, especially one who'd survived the rigors of medical school and residency, actually blushed? Be that as it may, that small flaw only enhanced her already attractive features.

Her fine bone structure gave her an ethereal quality, as if she didn't belong in a field as brutal as emergency medicine, but her athletic frame suggested she wasn't a stranger to hard work.

As lovely as he considered her face and form, her thick auburn hair was nothing short of awesome. The color reminded him of flames dancing on the hearth and without any effort at all he pictured her shaking out her braid until every strand cascaded over her beautiful shoulders.

If that wasn't enough, her shapely legs with their miles and miles of soft skin made his throat go dry. Today, like most days, she wore low-heeled pumps and a dress that fell to just above her slim knees. Her garb wasn't practical for the demands of working in Emergency and she'd probably switch to baggy scrub suits and tennis shoes tomorrow, but he'd enjoy the view while it lasted.

His libido and personal preferences aside, he was still glad she'd finally joined the emergency-services staff. For that reason, he found himself grinning like a loon whenever he saw her.

Actually, she hadn't *joined* as much as she'd been *transferred*. Over the past year, he'd created a paper blizzard that had gone to every department head, vice president and hospital-board member, protesting the fact that his department's extra medical position had never been filled. As soon as he'd learned of Sierra's credentials and past experience in Emergency, he'd intensified his efforts. If Administration had agreed they'd needed the position, he'd argued, then it was pointless not to fill it, especially when someone already on staff was ideal for the job.

While everyone agreed with his reasoning, Sierra's boss, Lane Keegan, hadn't wanted to lose her from the medical unit. If not for pressure from above, they'd still be at an impasse, but finally, after weeks of negotiating details, Keegan had given in. On one point, however, he'd refused to budge.

Sierra would only fill Trey's position until they found a replacement who met the criteria, but not for longer than sixty days. Which meant Trey still had fifty-nine to work his magic and convince her to stick around permanently. His philosophy was, *Better the devil you know than the one you don't,* and he'd prefer to keep Sierra, who got along well with the staff, rather than bring in a new person who might clash with everyone.

Roma Miller, the nursing supervisor who'd just received her thirty-year service pin, strode in. "Where was Dr. McAllaster going in such a hurry?"

He shrugged. "Lunch, I guess."

"No kidding? I've never seen her walk so fast."

Interesting. "She must be hungry," he offered, although he suspected the reason for her rush had had nothing to do with her appetite and everything to do with regaining her composure after he'd caught her studying him.

In spite of her cool attitude, in spite of her standoffish ways, Sierra McAllaster obviously wasn't as resistant to his charm as she pretended.

Munching on an apple, Sierra strolled along the circular concrete pathway of the hospital's favorite attraction—the Healing Garden and Labyrinth—which had been created just outside Emergency. Normally, she walked the circular concrete pathway in order to recharge her mental batteries when she had a tough patient, but today her reflections were far more personal and far more immediate.

Her ridiculous reaction to Trey's flattering comment still bothered her. Her marriage had taught her to not fall victim to a man's flattery and until now she hadn't. Why today was different remained a complete mystery. In her opinion, Trey's charm was a strike against him.

He had also earned a second strike because if it weren't for him, she'd still be reporting to work on the fifth floor, where she belonged. Although, in all fairness, she didn't know if she should be upset with him or with herself.

If she'd been in Trey's position, she would have presented the same case he had, asking that the vacant position be filled with a doctor who was already on staff and who possessed ED experience. As Fate would have it, she was the one with the least seniority—the only one, in fact—who fit the criteria.

Her options had been limited—either take this assignment or end her contract.

Leaving hadn't been a viable option. She'd finally unpacked the last box of household goods this past weekend and the idea of hunting for a new job was too tiring to contemplate.

On the other hand, she did have a third option. If she'd been honest and explained why she couldn't work in Emergency, perhaps Dr. Keegan might have chosen someone else. Pride, however, had stopped her. She'd come to Good Shepherd with a clean slate and if she dragged out her history to use like a get-out-of-jail-free card, her past would become an open book. The doubts, the pitying glances and every emotion in between would start, and she refused to deal with that from staff and her colleagues.

Consequently, she'd decided it might be time to face her fears and put those horrors behind her. Although she didn't *want* to work in Emergency, she suddenly had a desire to prove she was *able* to.

Fortunately, Dr. Keegan had offered her several consolation prizes. One—and the most important—she was only filling in temporarily. So what if she was back in the area where she'd sworn she'd never work again, treating everything from acid reflux to herpes zoster infections, traumas to diabetic comas? She'd endured far worse and for a far longer period. Sixty days was nothing more than a wrinkle that would iron itself out in due time.

Two, Dr. Keegan had promised she could return to her hospitalist position on the fifth floor. Knowing how the other internist, William Madison, was already complaining about covering those patients as well as his own in the cardiac ICU, he was also eager for her to shake the E.R. dust off her feet and return to where she belonged.

Three, the odds of encountering a trauma that involved a close friend or family member were nonexistent. After three months in Pittsburgh, she still hadn't developed any serious friendships or personal relationships and as long as she was expected to staff the ED, she intended to keep it that way.

As she strolled around the labyrinth, a growing sense of acceptance and her natural can-do attitude filled her. Her transfer may have thrown her off balance, but she was slowly feeling more in control over her situation. Today's trauma had only caused her a few moments of anticipatory dread, but after that she'd handled herself well. She'd still have some bad moments, but she'd be able to deal with them. She *would* deal with them.

Her next mental project was to get Trey Donovan, including his twinkling eyes and his lazy grin, out of her head. After a single morning in his presence, he'd already shattered her calm, making her wish for those happy-ever-afters she'd stopped imagining were possible.

She knew better than to respond like a schoolgirl to a man who had enough charisma for three guys, but she'd done it anyway. Maybe her reaction was due to first-day-on-a-new-job stress because she'd been dreading this day for the past week. Maybe it was because she hadn't slept well last night and her defenses were down.

Maybe it was because her blood sugar had dropped. She'd chosen to take the late lunch break and that had been delayed because they'd been busy.

Then again, maybe it was all of the above. Yes, she decided. That was it. She'd been simply tired, stressed and hungry. This afternoon, she'd be more like her old self, able to resist his wicked grins with the logic that they meant nothing.

"Can I walk with you?"

Startled out of her private thoughts, Sierra glanced down to see a girl, about ten years old, falling into step beside her on the concrete walkway. The child wore an oversize T-shirt, bright pink leggings and well-scuffed white-and-lavender tennis shoes. Her skin was tanned and her brown hair possessed lighter streaks, which suggested she spent a great deal of time outdoors. Several strands of hair had escaped her ponytail, which wasn't quite centered in the back of her head.

Although Sierra wanted to finish her walk through the labyrinth in contemplative quiet, she didn't want to be rude. Instead, she glanced around the garden, carefully scanning each bench for a potential parent or an otherwise responsible adult. Surprisingly, the garden was vacant and no one else was walking the labyrinth. They were alone.

"Won't your parents wonder where you are?" Sierra asked instead.

"My mom's dead and when my dad's out of town I stay with my uncle," the girl informed her. "He says I have to keep myself busy until he finishes his shift. He has a very important job, you know."

"Really?" she replied, amazed by how anyone could expect a child at her age to amuse herself in a hospital for hours on end. Surely a man who had this so-called "very important job" would realize that.

"He's a doctor," the child added meaningfully.

Sierra wasn't as impressed as the little girl obviously expected her to be. By virtue of his profession, the man should know better than to let a child run around a busy medical center completely unsupervised.

Immediately Sierra wondered if any of the physicians she knew had a niece this age, but none came to mind. Even so, something about this child's features seemed familiar.

"You're a doctor, too, aren't you?" the youngster asked, as if she already knew the answer.

"Yes, I am. Are you supposed to be outside by yourself?"

The girl drew herself up, adding an inch or so to her almost five-foot frame. "I'm almost eleven," she said, clearly affronted by Sierra's question. "My uncle says I can come out here if it's not raining." She raised her hands, palms up. "No rain today."

"No. No rain today," Sierra echoed. "Doesn't he worry about you wandering all over the hospital while he's working?"

"No, because I had to cross my heart…" she pantomimed "…and promise to follow the rules. I can only go to certain places, like the li-berry, the coffee shop or this garden. Or his office," she tacked on. "He trusts me."

At least this nameless man had set a few boundaries.

"The other rule is that I don't talk to or go with a stranger, no matter where I am."

"I'm a stranger," Sierra pointed out, deciding she would hunt down this irresponsible uncle and give him a piece of her mind, colleague or not! The risk was too great to leave this little girl unattended. The garden saw a lot of foot traffic and anyone who weighed more than a hundred pounds could haul this youngster off without breaking a sweat, even if she was kicking and screaming.

"No, you're not," she said, shaking her head. "I've seen you lots of times." She scurried in front of Sierra and peered at her identification badge. "You're Dr. McAllaster. Your name tag says so."

"Yes, but—"

"I'm Hannah," she answered. "Now we aren't strangers anymore."

Hannah's logic was definitely lacking. "Actually, we still are strangers," Sierra corrected her gently. "I could be a not-very-nice person."

Hannah's ponytail bounced with each shake of her head. "Nope, you're not. I've been watching you 'cause you come here almost as much as I do. If you were a rotten person, you wouldn't feed the birds your leftover crackers."

Goodness! Had she been so self-absorbed that she hadn't noticed an unattended child before today? Or maybe she'd seen her and thought she'd been under the watchful eye of one of the many visitors who came to the garden for fresh air and sunshine. Regardless, it was still eerie to realize that someone had observed her so carefully without her knowledge. She would definitely have to pay closer attention to her surroundings in the future.

"Plus, you're a doctor. Doctors aren't mean people. Oh, they can do nasty things like give us a shot, but it's for our own good," she said confidently.

While Sierra agreed that most physicians were caring individuals, she personally knew of several who should have chosen a different profession. Even so, she wouldn't destroy the girl's illusions. Life would take care of those soon enough.

"A lot of people come here to walk, don't they?" Hannah asked.

"They do."

"My uncle says they built this because the lab-y-rinth,"

she stumbled over the word, "is supposed to make people feel better. The Native Americans call it a medicine wheel."

"Really?"

"Uh-huh. They've gotten really popular, he says, especially at hospitals. Walking the path helps people who have stuff like high blood pressure or who can't relax. He says that the twists and turns are s'posed to represent the twists and turns in life."

The child sounded like a brochure that detailed the hospital's services. "He's right. The labyrinth helps people put the bad things in perspective."

"Is that why you're here? So you can put the bad stuff in pers...pers...pective?"

Hannah's insight surprised her. Sierra began visiting the garden during her lunch hour as part of her mental-health regimen when she'd first joined the medical staff. Walking the circular concrete pathways, which were lined with colorful petunias, helped her deal with stress, especially after she lost a patient. She also knew of several surgeons who walked the labyrinth in order to clear their heads before performing surgery.

"Yes, I do," Sierra said. "Why do *you* come here? To be outdoors instead of being cooped up inside?"

Hannah shrugged. "I like this place. My mom died of cancer when I was little, and whenever I get sad, I walk until I feel better. Do you think she might have lived if there'd been a lab-y-rinth at her hospital?"

Hannah's matter-of-fact tone didn't minimize the compassion Sierra felt for her. Oddly enough, she almost wanted to give her nameless uncle a break. Being a single parent or, in this case, an uncle wasn't easy, especially when one dealt with an obviously precocious child like Hannah.

"Sometimes cancer wins, no matter how hard people try to fight it."

Hannah's brown eyebrows drew together as she nodded. "That's what my uncle says, too. He says she didn't want to die, but it wasn't her fault she couldn't stay and watch me grow up."

"No, it wasn't," Sierra agreed.

Oddly enough, her uncle seemed to have imparted good insight to his niece. Sierra added one mental point in his favor.

Suddenly, the sound of dogs barking broke the quiet. Hannah immediately pulled a hot-pink cell phone out of the matching pouch hanging around her neck and the barking stopped. Sierra chuckled at herself as she realized the noise was a ringtone instead of a pack of canines on the loose.

The youngster glanced at the display and winced. "Gotta go. 'Bye!"

"Wait!" Sierra called as Hannah began hurdling the flowers with an easy-limbed grace in her haste to head toward the north door. "What's your uncle's name?"

Hannah simply smiled and waved before she disappeared through the north door.

So much for discovering the child's identity, Sierra thought as she watched Hannah somewhat benevolently. Knowing Hannah had a cell phone made her feel somewhat better about the situation.

To Sierra's disappointment, her wristwatch showed her allotted break time was over, too, even though she hadn't reached the center of the labyrinth. After taking one last look in Hannah's direction and seeing her disappear through the glass entrance doors, Sierra carefully stepped over the petunias as she strode in the opposite direction and disposed of her apple core in the trash.

Inside the main emergency hallway, ringing telephones, whispering gurney wheels and excited voices contrasted sharply with the tranquility she'd left behind. Directly ahead, she saw two different paramedics from the ones she'd met earlier, another ED physician and a nurse escorting another gurney into a trauma room. Meanwhile, Trey was heading toward an exam room as he reviewed the form on his clipboard. As soon as he saw her, his smile widened.

"How was lunch?" he asked.

She thought of the precocious Hannah. "Interesting. Why don't I take over for you so you can take your break?"

"Thanks, but this case shouldn't take too long. It's also too early to meet my lunch date in the cafeteria, so I might as well earn my pay."

She should have known. The man probably arranged his personal schedule months ahead. "Then I won't keep you."

Before she turned away, he stopped her. "Save tomorrow for me, though."

She paused. "Excuse me?"

"Lunch. Tomorrow. My treat. It'll be my official 'welcome to the department' gesture."

"Do you take every new person to lunch?" she asked.

"Everyone," he reassured her. "Even the housekeeping staff. So don't pack your apple."

She stared at him in surprise. "How did you know—?"

"I'm an observant kind of guy."

Of course he was, she thought wryly. "Okay, fine. We'll do lunch." Then, to make certain there would be no misunderstandings, she added, "Strictly between colleagues."

His smile seemed as broad as his shoulders. "Fair enough."

She turned away, but he stopped her. "Out of curiosity, are you seeing anyone?"

This time she smiled. "What does the grapevine say?"

"You're not."

"Correct, as usual," she agreed lightly.

"Is there someone back home?" he pressed.

Sierra hesitated. How could she explain, and did she want to? However, if her answer prevented speculation and stopped people from pushing her towards every eligible man who came along, why not?

"There was," she replied slowly.

"Breakups are tough," he agreed, his expression sympathetic. "So you came to Pittsburgh to start over?"

If only it had been that simple. "I did, but the situation is a little more complicated than a mere breakup." She met his gaze. "When I left North Carolina, I left my husband in the Fairview Cemetery."

CHAPTER TWO

TREY didn't know what had possessed him to broach the subject of her personal life. Perhaps he'd simply been looking for an excuse to stay away from Sierra and hearing of a fellow back home would have provided it. Perhaps he was simply a glutton for punishment and hearing of her unattached status would only provide a temptation he'd be hard-pressed to resist.

Unfortunately, her response had been completely unexpected. He'd certainly never dreamed that the man she'd left behind had been her husband, much less that he was *dead*.

Certainly, the information she'd shared explained so much—her long hours, her avoidance of the dating scene, and her move to a new city and work environment. She hadn't come to Pittsburgh on some grand adventure to see the world. Like his brother, Mitch. Sierra was picking up the pieces of her life.

All of which proved his theory—the best relationships were temporary.

"I'm sorry," he murmured.

She nodded, apparently accustomed to hearing condolences if her frozen expression was any indication. "Thanks," she murmured. Then, with a visibly shaky hand she smoothed her hair. "Are you sure you wouldn't like me to see your patient?"

Her abrupt change of subject couldn't have been more plain. Their question-and-answer period had come to a close, which was good. For a man who never had trouble find-ing something to talk about, he was suddenly at a loss for words.

He glanced at his watch. He only had ten minutes before his cafeteria appointment and it took nearly seven to walk there. "Do you mind?"

"Not at all. Enjoy your lunch."

Eager to get away before he asked more questions, Sierra pulled the clipboard out of his hand and headed down the hall. She'd already shared more than she'd ever planned, and if she gave him enough time, the inevitable "What happened?" would follow.

She simply didn't want to go there. Not now. Not yet. The tragedy had occurred over a year ago and she simply refused to dredge up those old feelings of shock, despair and anger, not to mention guilt. She'd finally come to the acceptance stage, but it hadn't been easy.

Now, however, was not the time to walk down memory lane and analyze the past. At the moment, the only person who deserved her full attention was her patient—not Trey Donovan, and certainly not David McAllaster.

By the time she'd received the results of Karen Maxwell's strep screen—it was negative—and referred her to an ENT specialist to evaluate her chronic sinusitis, Trey had returned, looking as rested and refreshed as he had before their full morning of traumas and regular patients.

As Sierra sank onto a chair in the nurses' station, she noticed he was chatting up one of the radiology techs. The poor girl was smiling as if he'd single-handedly hung the sun, moon and stars.

"He has quite a knack with the women, doesn't he?" Sierra mused aloud to Roma, who was clicking away on her key-board at a nearby terminal.

"You must be talking about our famous Dr. Donovan," Roma answered, without glancing away from her screen.

"How did you guess?"

"He does have a way with people," she commented. "Young, old, male, female, staff, patients, it doesn't matter. Why, I've seen him talk the most recalcitrant patients into behaving. When he's on duty, things just run more smoothly."

Sierra understood why. By virtue of his personality, he inspired people to dig deeply and give one-hundred-and-ten percent.

Just like David.

The only question was, did Trey do it for personal gain, or was he as altruistic as everyone believed? She wasn't quite convinced of the latter.

Roma finally glanced away from her screen to direct her gaze down the hallway. "He's so sweet to all of us. In fact, everyone fancies themselves a bit in love with him," she remarked.

"I've gotten that impression," Sierra said wryly. "Given the way women act when he's around, I'd bet he never spends an evening alone. I'm surprised he has the energy to come to work."

The nurse laughed. "There's where you're wrong. He doesn't date as often as you might think. Oh, there are a lot who'd give their right arm for a night with him, but he's very careful about who he takes out. And he never sees anyone more than a handful of times."

"Really." Sierra wasn't convinced, but Roma seemed to know what she was talking about. "I find that hard to believe."

Roma shrugged. "It's true. Dr. Donovan seems like a happy-go-lucky sort, but don't let his winning ways fool you. There's a lot more to our good doctor than meets the eye."

Sierra watched as the X-ray tech walked away with a light step, her face beaming in obvious delight over her encounter with Trey. Meanwhile, he wore his own satisfied expression, which suggested he'd gotten whatever he'd wanted.

Just like David, she thought with some disgust. Everything was a game, nobody was anything more than a chess piece.

Thank goodness she'd grown wise to such manipulations. She'd been a pawn once in her life. She wouldn't be one again.

After finishing with his next patient, Trey strode back to the doctors' office. He'd requested a CT scan for one of his patients with a debilitating headache and Lila, the X-ray tech, had promised the images would be online by two o'clock. It was five minutes till, so he didn't expect to see them posted, but it didn't hurt to check.

He accessed Joan Villiers's computer file and, as he'd suspected, the CT scan was still pending. A brisk knock at the door heralded Roma's arrival.

"I've been looking all over for you," the nurse remarked as she entered.

"What's up?"

"Frances is here."

"What's wrong today?"

"Stomachache. Do you want me to give her to Dr. McAllaster?"

He thought a moment. "Yeah, but I'd better introduce them first, don't you think?"

"Probably. Although I think the introductions are more for Dr. McAllaster's benefit than Frances's."

"Right as usual." Because he was curious, he asked, "From a nursing point of view, what's your opinion of our new doc?"

Roma didn't hesitate. "I think she's doing okay. She's a little tense, especially during traumas, but other than that I don't have any complaints."

"It's her first day," he reminded her. "She's bound to be a little tense."

"Hey, I wasn't finding fault," Roma protested. "Only making an observation which, as you said, is only to be expected. Now, if she'd come in all cocky and acting like a know-it-all, then I'd worry." She patted Trey's shoulder. "You done good, Doc, when you convinced them to transfer her to us."

Pleased by Roma's praise, he smiled. "I did, didn't I?"

"According to the nurses on the fifth floor, they're extremely upset because we stole her away."

"It's only for sixty days." More or less.

"Yeah, well, they're afraid they won't get her back. According to them, she knows her stuff. Better yet, and unlike some doctors who shall remain nameless, she doesn't treat them like they're too stupid to live."

"We were fortunate she came to Good Shepherd," he commented, keeping the story Sierra had shared to himself. If she wanted everyone to know she was a widow—and she obviously didn't if the information hadn't circulated on the grapevine—she could divulge that news herself.

"Rumor says she didn't want to be assigned to the E.R.," Roma pointed out. "As you're the one responsible for her transfer, I hope you intend to turn on the charm until she settles in."

"Hey, I only made the suggestion," he protested. "The decision came from people above my pay grade."

"Be that as it may, if you hadn't pushed for her, she wouldn't be here."

Roma was right. If he hadn't waged his one-man war, his department would still be suffering from the lack of a physician. "Probably not," he agreed. "We were lucky the upper echelon saw the situation from our point of view."

Roma sighed. "I wish she'd applied for the E.R. post in the first place. Everything would be settled. As it is, who knows what her replacement will be like?"

The same thought had crossed Trey's mind on several occasions. "I'm hoping she'll grow to love us and will stay."

"Hope all you want," Roma said darkly, "but given how other physicians feel about E.R. docs, my money says she'll run back to the fifth floor as soon as she can."

Not if he could help matters… "I assume you're referring to how the rest of the physicians look down on us because of the popular belief that we only decide on whether or not to admit a patient."

"Yeah."

It was a common stereotype, thanks to the nature of his profession. The people who presented themselves were either bleeding or sick and it was his job to either cure them or pass them off to someone who could, doing both as fast as possible. The department wasn't called Emergency for nothing. Being the metropolitan city that Pittsburgh was, their ED never had a dull moment.

"We may not have an official client list like a private practice does, but we definitely have our regulars," he mentioned.

"Like Frances."

"Like Frances," he echoed. "A lot of people list us as their primary-care physicians."

"Probably," Roma agreed, "but I'll bet Dr. McAllaster feels as if she's taken a step down in her career. Mind you, the nurses have a saying. 'If the doctor ain't happy, then nobody's happy.'"

Trey disagreed. So far, Sierra hadn't lost her temper or raised her voice and she'd been in various situations where it wouldn't have been inappropriate. While staying calm was a great trait to exhibit in an emergency situation, over the past few months of their quasi working relationship, from what he'd seen, the woman gave the word *unflappable* new meaning.

"I think you're wrong," he said. "Sierra is too classy a lady to take out her frustrations on the rest of us."

"She might be classy, but redheads can have fiery tempers."

As far as he was concerned, calling Sierra a redhead was like describing the Perseid meteor shower as a few shooting stars, or the Grand Canyon as a big hole in the ground. "I'm not sure one has anything to do with the other. I've known lots of hot-tempered brunettes and blondes, too."

"Okay, so I'm stereotyping," she admitted, "but we'll see fireworks down here before it's over."

He was half-eager for Roma's fears to come true. Sierra, with her brown eyes flashing with the same fire he saw in her hair, would be an awesome sight. "Fireworks can be beautiful."

"Yeah, in the night sky off the Roberto Clemente Bridge. Not in the hospital and without any warning."

"I thought you liked to live life dangerously."

"Me? Mrs. Boring who's married to Mr. Extremely Boring?" She shook her head, smiling. "Not a chance. As much as I like my job, it has enough inherent aggravation without me looking for trouble. Speaking of which, the sooner we take care of Frances, the better."

"Okay, but I have to check my CT scan result first. If everything looks okay and the injection we gave Mrs. Villiers is working, we can send her home." A few keystrokes later, he found his report and read it with satisfaction. "Sure enough. She can go."

After sharing his news with Mrs. Villiers, Trey found Sierra at the nurses' station, ready to grab another clipboard out of the in-box.

"Before you take that case, I have a person I want you to meet," he told her. "Room Ten."

"A patient?"

How could he describe Frances? "Yes and no," he admitted.

Her answering chuckle sounded sweet. "Which is it?" she asked.

"Frances is one of our colorful regulars. She's a twenty-five-year-old woman with a learning disability who lives about a block away. Her mother used to work here and so she understands that the Good Shepherd E.R. is where people come for help."

"Okay, so what's unusual?"

"When I refer to 'help,' I'm using an extremely broad definition."

"How broad is broad?"

"She comes in for minor things like a sliver in her hand, a skinned knee or a broken blister. She usually goes straight to the triage nurse, who finds out what she needs. Then, the nurse sends her to me or to one of the other doctors if I'm busy. We give her a little TLC and send her on her way."

"I assume that I'm 'one of the other doctors'?" she said dryly.

"Do you mind?"

"Not at all."

"Good, because if you ever do see her, her visit will go easier if I've introduced you."

"Okay. What's her complaint?"

"Stomachache."

She glanced at his empty hands. "Where's her paper-work?"

"We don't create any."

Sierra stared at Trey. "No paper trail?"

"Like I said, she comes relatively often with such minor problems that we'd waste more time filling out forms than if we'd actually deal with her situation."

She'd been warned of Trey Donovan's unorthodox style, but she hadn't expected to find an example of it so quickly.

"A few administrative people might be upset by the way you're handling this individual," she commented cautiously, to test his response. "Treating a patient without documentation. Legal liability issues, etcetera."

He shrugged as if he was unconcerned. "I suppose they might be unhappy if Frances sues us for not removing a splinter properly. Until then, I guess you'll have to decide if you'll keep our secret or not."

Sierra ignored the challenge in his voice. "Have you encouraged her to visit the outpatient clinic instead of the E.R.?"

"Frances has come here since she was a little girl so the concept is ingrained in her. Do *you* want to try and change her belief system at this late date?

"Besides," he continued, "the clinic staff doesn't know her like we do. They won't take time for the minor things and if they do, they certainly won't operate out of the goodness of their hearts. She won't understand when they turn her away or ask her to pay, and then she'll get upset and fall apart, which I can assure you is not a pretty sight. It saves so much wear and tear on everyone if we just do what needs to be done. A regular win-win situation."

Sierra wanted to argue that Frances's caseworker needed to be involved, but several things stopped her.

One, she was intrigued by how the ED staff had literally taken this woman under their wing.

Two, this was Trey's domain. As the most senior ED physician, he knew his department's strengths and limitations far better than she did. He also had the authority to establish policies and procedures, with or without his immediate supervisor's approval. If he wanted to handle Frances in his own way, he certainly had the clout to do so.

This also seemed to be a prime opportunity to either build a bridge or a brick wall. She could stick to the hospital rule book, which would earn her brownie points from her superiors, or she could save her energy for more important battles.

On the other hand, if she caved in on this issue, was she setting a precedent? What if ten more people like Frances decided to visit the E.R. for their scrapes and scratches? They'd never have time or space to deal with the heart attacks, the broken bones or the car wrecks.

Would turning a blind eye signal that she was a pushover for a heartwarming story or a special case? The argument could be made that *every* person coming through the doors had special circumstances necessitating unusual solutions.

Can't you be flexible for once in your life?

David's voice whispered the last question and she instinctively stiffened. Unfortunately, his concept of flexibility had been his excuse for taking advantage of every opportunity that had come his way—opportunities that had covered everything from his business activities to moral decisions.

She'd always prided herself on meeting the needs of her patients, so how was this any different? If Frances had been one of *her* regular clients, would she have chosen differently than Trey and his staff had?

She let out a breath and nodded. "Let's see Frances."

Before she could take a step forward, he stopped her.

"If it looks like she has something serious, I want you to take over."

"Why?"

"Because if I'm busy holding her hand to keep her calm, I can't do my doctor thing."

She chuckled at his choice of words. "Can't walk and chew gum at the same time, eh?"

He rolled his eyes melodramatically. "Ah, *now* she makes a joke."

"Sorry," she said, unrepentant, "I couldn't help it. Okay, we'll do it your way. I'll examine her while you play nursemaid. From what I've seen so far, you're pretty good at hand-holding and sweet-talking."

His grin was boyishly wicked. "I'm good at other things, too."

The sudden flare of heat in his eyes spoke of more physical activities—activities that her imagination so unhelpfully supplied in vivid, living color.

If she was going to work with the delectable Dr. D. so closely over the next few months, she really would have to get more sleep. Exhaustion didn't give her the mental fortitude to rein in her wayward thoughts.

"I'm sure you are," she said lightly.

Inside the room, Sierra saw the dark-haired woman curled into a fetal position on the bed. Another nurse, Billie, was taking her vital signs.

"Hi, Franny," Trey said as he approached the bed and immediately took her pulse. "I hear you're not feeling well today."

Frances opened her eyes and offered a weak smile. "Hi Dr. D.," she said in a singsong voice. "My stomach really, really hurts bad. Can you fix it?"

Her childlike question made Sierra wish for the several-hundredth time that medicine could solve the problem of a child's mind trapped inside an adult body. Not many people could deal effectively with people with learning disabilities, and she carefully watched Trey's demeanor. She didn't know what she was expecting, but she was pleasantly surprised to watch him smile benevolently at Frances while he patted her arm and questioned her about her diet.

As he talked, she herself focused on his sinfully thick dark hair, dark eyes and long eyelashes. She'd never studied him up close and personal before, but she understood how he'd developed his reputation of a dreamboat.

Thank goodness she wasn't taken in by appealing packages.

"I think I was poisoned," Frances moaned.

"Her temp is one-oh-two," Billie interjected.

Trey glanced at Sierra, his humor evident in his eyes. "I don't think you have food poisoning, Frances. But you are sick, which makes me glad I brought our very best doctor to see you. This is Dr. McAllaster."

Sierra took her cue to come forward. "Hi, Frances."

Frances gazed at Trey. "She can't be the best 'cause you are."

He chuckled. "Thanks, Franny, but stomachaches are Dr. McAllaster's specialty. Will you let her examine you?"

Frances apparently was convinced because she slowly nodded. "If you say so."

Sierra immediately took over, not surprised by Trey's ability to gain Frances's cooperation. He'd obviously been dealing with this woman for quite a while.

"Okay, Frances," she said softly. "I need you to stretch out for me."

"But it hurts when I do," she wailed.

"I know, but I really need you to lie flat." After much

maneuvering and moaning, Sierra gently prodded Frances's abdomen. It didn't take long to decide that her problem didn't have a simple solution.

She turned to Trey. "Do you remember the paperwork you said you didn't initiate? You'd better start it now."

Over the next hour, Sierra realized she couldn't have done her job without Trey. While Frances's problem had been fairly straightforward, it had taken longer to arrive at the diagnosis because she hadn't been particularly cooperative. Thank goodness Trey was a salesman at heart. He explained, gave guarantees and promised her everything from watching television to an ice cream if she'd allow them to do one more test.

He saw Frances through the pain of bloodwork and he did so with patience she hadn't expected—patience that wasn't contrived.

Neither did he express any great relief to relinquish his task when Frances's mother arrived. Instead, he simply changed gears from moral-support agent to physician as easily as he flashed his handsome smile.

"Appendicitis?" he asked as soon as he cornered Sierra at the nurses' station.

"I'm impressed," she said, amazed at how he'd pinpointed her diagnosis before they'd received any reports. "You really can walk and chew gum at the same time."

"What can I say? I'm a man of many talents. Plus, it didn't take too much effort to add lower-right-quadrant pain and rebound tenderness with a fever to come up with appendicitis. I assume her white count is elevated?"

"According to the report that came through a minute ago, it's eighteen point four. I've already called Vijay. He said because it's such a clear-cut case to save him a trip and send her upstairs to surgery."

Vijay Gupta was a fourth-year surgical resident assigned to Emergency. Sierra had consulted with him on several patients prior to her current E.R. stint and thought highly of him. After he completed his training, he planned to return to his native India and Sierra would be sorry to see him go.

"Sounds good to me."

Sierra always took pride in making accurate and timely diagnoses, but none more so than when Trey stopped her a few hours later, not long before their shift ended.

"Vijay called," he said without preamble. "Frances's appendix was the worst he's seen in a long time. You'll be pleased to know he was glad you'd sent her up when you did, otherwise there would have been dire consequences."

Gracious, but she was blushing again. "It was a team effort," she said lightly.

"That may be, but I think we should celebrate with a cup of coffee."

"Coffee sounds good, but I'm not sure the occasion calls for a celebration," she said. "I was only doing my job."

The second those words came out of her mouth she realized how much she'd sounded like Professor "Grumpy" Gunderson. After she'd pored over a patient's medical file for clues about his illness, she'd discovered an obscure fact which had led to a confirmatory test. Her fellow students had been impressed and she'd been proud, but "Grumpy" had raised one eyebrow and sniffed.

"You're *expected* to make proper diagnoses, McAllaster," he'd said in his most condescending voice. "*Every* patient deserves your best. It's your job to provide it."

Now, a question begged to be asked. When had she become so cynical and turned into Grumpy Gunderson?

"Working down here..." Trey interrupted her bleak thoughts as he herded her into the lounge "...we take our victories when we find them. Too many cases don't have happy endings."

As if she'd needed a reminder, she reflected wryly as he began pouring two mugs of the strong coffee.

"Black or white?" he asked.

"White." She fished among the containers for a packet of

sweetener and dumped in a moderate amount of powdered creamer.

He leaned against the counter, mug in hand. "Just so you know, our real partying takes place on Fridays, after work. You'll have to join us. No excuses allowed."

She thought about the days when she'd ended the work week with the rest of her ED team at a nearby watering hole. Their tradition had been for the most senior member to make two toasts—one to the staff for jobs well done and one to pay tribute to the people they'd lost.

Her finances could surely stretch far enough for her to resume the tradition, even if she honored it only during her temporary tenure in Emergency. While she took pride in her efforts when she'd discharged a patient from the fifth floor, drinking a glass of wine alone in her apartment didn't generate the same emotional satisfaction as being surrounded by people who'd shared in the experience.

Until Trey had dangled the notion of a celebration in front of her, she hadn't realized how much she missed the camaraderie associated with a group of her colleagues. Trey had inadvertently reminded her of another part of her life that David had stolen.

Well, no more. She'd come to Pittsburgh to start over, and creating a new routine was part of that. She may not be able to afford more than a glass of tea or a soft drink, but drinking wasn't the issue. Being with friends and colleagues was.

"I didn't realize I'd touched on such a deep subject," he joked. "You looked like you were a hundred miles away."

"Sorry," she said, embarrassed at being caught woolgathering. "I was, but you're right. We should rejoice in our success stories when we can."

His smile nearly blinded her. "Then you'll join us on Friday night?"

"Sure, why not?"

"Great," he said with such enthusiasm that she knew he'd hold her to her decision, no matter what. "We'll—"

Their pagers went off simultaneously. Sierra abandoned her mug and followed Trey out of the door.

A scuffle at the far end of the hall near the ambulance entrance doors caught her attention. Two police officers were escorting two punks in low-slung jeans and ripped T-shirts, but for every step forward they sidestepped two more in an effort to keep the two street hoods apart. Obscenities flew, along with several wild punches, but it was obvious that not long ago those punches had been landing.

One young man had a swollen, bloody nose and a blood-stained bandana wrapped around his right biceps. The other had one eye completely swollen shut as he limped forward.

Trey sighed. "Looks like the natives are restless."

"No kidding. I thought they saved their fighting for Saturday nights," she remarked.

"Around here, any time is a good time," he answered. "I'll take one and you can take the other so we can get them both out of here faster."

"Okay."

She started forward, but he pulled her behind him. "Stay out of the way until they're stashed in separate corners."

Stay out of the way? For a few seconds she stood in amazement at his high-handedness. Did he really think she couldn't hold her own? She'd gone nose to nose with men who were far more belligerent than these two. Of course, she hadn't been wearing a dress and heels at the time, but sometimes looking feminine gave her an advantage. Goons like these were often busy ogling her legs and forgot their reason for fighting.

She hurried to catch up, but Trey's long-legged stride had already put him at the scene. Although she was still half a hallway away, she heard and saw everything.

"Take him…" Trey pointed to the one sporting a bloody nose "…to Trauma One and the other to Room Two."

"Move it, buddy." Officer Wright gave his prisoner a not-so-gentle nudge in the appropriate direction. "You heard the doc."

"Hey, man, don't tell me what to do." The guy immediately began swinging.

Instinctively, Sierra knew this wasn't going to end well. She watched in horror as the situation deteriorated, taking Trey with it.

CHAPTER THREE

TREY saw the man's arm move out of the corner of his eye. He tried to duck as he watched a beefy fist come toward him, but his body didn't respond to his brain's command. His instincts warned him of the impending blow, but before he had a chance to brace himself for impact, his ears rang and his vision blurred.

He heard shouts and curses as if they were coming from a distance, but he concentrated on trying to protect himself. Before his scrambled brain could convince him to duck, a body plowed into his midsection and he lost his balance. His fall inevitable, he twisted to minimize the damage, but five hundred pounds of angry males landed on top of him, effectively causing him to kiss the floor.

The bruise on his chin and the weight on his back seemed minor in comparison to the excruciating pain that he felt in his right knee.

Damn! This wasn't how this was supposed to play out, he thought, before everything faded to black.

Before Sierra could yell at Trey to watch out for the guy on his right, she heard the distinctive sound of flesh striking bone. For a split second, he stood upright, frozen in place, until the other man shoved Trey in his apparent haste to reach his enemy. Immediately, Trey crumpled like a broken toy and disappeared under the bodies of punks and police officers.

"Call Security," she yelled over her shoulder as she hurried forward. She certainly couldn't fight this battle if she relied on muscle because she was definitely outgunned. However, she could win through chemistry.

"Lorazepam," she called out, already calculating an appropriate dose of tranquilizer to use. "Hand me lorazepam!"

Suddenly, what seemed like the entire emergency department materialized around them. By the time someone had slapped the medication in her hand, there were too many arms and legs to identify the owners. She could accidentally sedate a staff member, which would definitely not be the best thing to do.

To her great frustration, she simply had to wait for stronger backs to peel back the pile, layer by layer. Finally, only Trey was lying facedown on the floor.

Sierra knelt beside him, half-afraid of what she might find. "Trey," she said urgently as she frantically ran her fingers over his head to check for injuries. "Can you hear me?"

She found a goose egg on his forehead, presumably caused by his bounce against the linoleum. "Trey?" she asked again.

This time, he groaned. "Must you scream in my ear?" he complained.

He'd answered. What a relief. "I'm not screaming. Can you move?"

"Barely." He grimaced as he tried to roll over and only got as far as his side. "Damn. My knee."

She placed a hand on his shoulder to steady him. "Anything else?"

"You mean, other than the fact that my lungs will never be the same after being squashed within an inch of my life?"

She smiled at his affronted tone. If he could be sarcastic, his injuries probably weren't as bad as she'd feared. His skin color was on the pasty side, but he didn't sound wheezy or raspy, which was good because she felt guilty enough for not wading into the fray with him. "Yeah, other than that."

"You're the doc. You tell me."

She paused to study him with her practiced eye. "We'll

need X-rays to check for hairline skull fractures or broken ribs, but as a purely preliminary opinion I'd cancel any photo ops if I were you."

He swiped at the blood running down his chin. "That bad, eh?"

"It could be worse," she said, taking a gauze pad someone had handed her to hold against his chin. "Besides the goose egg that's probably giving you a headache and the gash you're already well acquainted with, you're developing quite a shiner. Don't worry, though. You'll be back to your handsome self in no time."

"My handsome self, eh?" He tried to grin, but it came out as a grimace. With shaky fingers, he gently probed his cheekbone. "Oh, that hurts."

"I'm sure. Pain is a common side effect of having your face meet a fist, but ice will help. What about your chest? Can you breathe in and out easily?"

He huffed first, then took a deep breath and let it out. "Yeah." He rubbed the side of his chest. "My ribs are sore, though. How do football players handle this day after day?"

"Conditioning and extra padding," she answered. "Let's get you to a room so I can look at your knee. Ready?"

He winced. "I'll have to be."

Immediately, multiple hands pulled him upright. "Any dizziness?" she asked.

"Not really," he muttered as he sank heavily into a waiting wheelchair, his face white with pain.

"Who's on call for Orthopedics?" Sierra asked Roma.

"Abernathy. I'll page him," the nurse said.

She turned back to Trey. "Ready for your ride down the hall?"

"No. I want to go home instead."

"Don't be a baby," she scolded lightly as she pushed his wheelchair alongside a bevy of worried-looking staff.

"Did anyone ever tell you your bedside manner lacks a little something?" he grumbled. "Like compassion?"

"Would you rather I stand here and gush all over you?" she wanted to know. "If so, I could hand you to another doctor, but I don't think Lamont or Ben are likely to treat you like spun glass either. Marissa might, but you're older than her usual clientele, so who knows?"

Lamont Stedman and Benjamin Kryszka, both men pushing forty, were the other two ED physicians on duty. Marissa Landower, an attractive woman about ten years older, was the resident pediatrician. While any of them would fuss a bit over him, none would fall apart like a dewy-eyed debutante.

He peered at her, looking like a lopsided raccoon. "I should get hazardous-duty pay."

"If it will make you feel better, I'll give you one of the kids' sugar-free lollipops. Cherry or grape?"

"Can you lace it with a painkiller?" he asked, his voice hopeful.

"Sorry."

"Then I'll pass."

Sierra braked the wheelchair beside the bed. "Do you want to hop up here or stay where you are?"

"I'll stay right here, thank you very much. It'll save on wear and tear when you send me to my car. So I can go home," he finished pointedly.

"What? And miss a trip to Radiology?" She tutted. "Now, Dr. Donovan—"

"This is so unnecessary," he grumbled. "I have a minor bump on my head, my chin's not bleeding nearly as badly as it was and I wrenched my knee. Nothing that a few ice packs and a bandage won't cure."

She leaned over to study the gash, fully aware of how wonderful he smelled. "You're right about your chin. A butterfly bandage should take care of it. As for the rest of your aches, we need X-rays."

"No, we don't."

His expression reminded her of a little boy whose wishes were being thwarted. If he crossed his arms and stuck out his lower lip, the picture would be complete.

The diagnosis was in and it was definite—Dr. Donovan was a lousy patient.

"Yes, we do," she said, hiding her amusement. "How would it look if I sent you home with a subdural hematoma, a concussion or a torn ACL?"

"I didn't tear my ACL," he said. "Anterior cruciate ligament tears would be more painful and I would have heard a distinct pop, which I didn't. I also didn't fracture my skull and I absolutely, positively, do not have a concussion."

"Here's your ice pack, Doctor." A nurse thrust the cold bag at him and he placed it on his face with heartfelt thanks.

"You know your brain wasn't scrambled because…?" She waited for his response.

"I've had a concussion before and my current headache doesn't come close."

"That's good to hear, but while you may have Superman's X-ray vision, I, as your physician, do not." She motioned to one of the nurses to begin taking his vital signs. "So your opinion is overruled. We might even spring for an MRI of your knee."

"You're making far too much of this."

"Risk Management and Workman's Comp all require a thorough exam, which is what I'm trying to do. As one of the hospital's finest and most illustrious staff members, you should sit back and enjoy the attention."

"I'd rather be at home, licking my wounds in private."

While his injuries were obviously painful, she suspected they were strictly of the minor variety. "You'll get there soon enough," she predicted. "Meanwhile, let's slip you into a hospital gown so we can take a look at—"

"Not a chance."

"It's either that or cut off your pants leg," she warned. "I can't see through fabric either."

"Grab your scissors," he said firmly. "Losing a pair of pants is not worth the indignity."

"Okay, but it's a waste of a perfectly good garment."

"They're mine to waste. Cut."

With an order like that, she couldn't refuse. She began snipping through the cotton, careful to avoid puncturing his skin. Each slice revealed more of his muscular leg and caused her mouth to suddenly go dry.

To make matters worse, she was oddly unsettled by her task, which was ridiculous because she'd cut off clothing before without a second thought, and on a number of men more handsome than Trey. If she wasn't almost finished, she would have turned over the job to one of the hovering nurses, who clearly would have been thrilled at the honor.

"Do you run?" she asked, trying to deal with her view of his leg clinically.

"Yeah."

His knee was too swollen for her to pull the free leg off, so she sliced the fabric lengthwise and laid it open. "You'll have to postpone your daily jogs for a while."

"You think?"

She smiled at his sarcasm. "You really are holding true to the stereotype about doctors being lousy patients."

"I'm entitled. This whole thing was so *stupid!* It should never have happened."

The guilt she'd been holding at bay reappeared. "Maybe next time you'll let me handle it."

His battered face didn't hide his skepticism. "And what would you have done? Ended up at the bottom of the pile with me? Or, worse yet, *instead* of me?"

His outrage was obvious and she understood why. Men hated appearing weak. Being caught off guard and injured because of a misplaced punch would, in their opinion, epitomize the very trait they hated. Now, if he'd earned his wounds because he'd thrown a few blows of his own, they would have become badges of honor.

"Maybe you're right," she conceded, "but you shouldn't feel embarrassed either. In fact, once news gets out, you'll become more popular than you already are."

"I guess." He didn't sound too happy about his new status,

which surprised her. David had always preened under extra attention and she'd expected Trey to do the same.

"Can I have some ibuprofen and ice for my knee now?" he complained.

"The ice is coming right up," she said. "We'll save the pain reliever until after your CT scan."

"BP is one forty-five over eighty," the nurse broke in to report. "Pulse is sixty-eight."

"Your blood pressure is a little high—"

"Of course it is," he snapped. "Getting caught in the middle of a fight will do that."

Sierra exchanged a wry glance with Roma. Clearly the charge nurse held Sierra's opinion about Trey's attitude. She looked as if she was ready to comment when another nurse brought a fresh ice pack, breaking the moment.

Sierra secured the bag to his knee with elastic wrap. "This'll hold it in place while you're visiting Radiology. After you're back and Dr. Abernathy sees you, we'll wrap your knee more securely."

"What? No Lachman's? No pivot shift test?"

She smiled as he referred to the two tests performed to diagnose an ACL injury. "Knowing an orthopedist will do those himself, do you really want me to manipulate your knee and leg just to prove I know how?"

"True. Good idea to wait."

Sierra stepped aside. "I'll see you when you get back."

For the next hour, past the time Sierra's shift should have ended, a steady stream of staff members approached her to ask how Trey was doing. Even the people who were just reporting for duty had heard of the mishap and begged for details.

The two prisoners stopped her in the hallway to gruffly pass on their apologies to Trey before their caretakers herded them to jail.

"What was all that about?" she asked Ben and Lamont, who acted rather pleased with themselves as they perched on the counter beside her.

"We let it be known they'd better be on their best behavior if they ever come here again because we don't take kindly to our staff getting hurt," Lamont replied. "The next time they lose their cool and need something more than a few stitches, we'll use drugs that produce some unpleasant side effects."

"Like impotence, incontinence, hair loss, skin blemishes, boils, diarrhea and blurred vision," Ben chimed in.

"Not to mention anal leakage and flatulence."

Sierra looked at her two colleagues in amazement. "You didn't."

"We did," Lamont assured her, before he exchanged a wide grin with his partner-in-crime.

She laughed. "You guys are awful. You both look so meek and mild-mannered, but underneath you have an evil streak."

"Hey," Lamont protested without heat, "we protect our own. Now that we've done our good deed for the day, we're going home. Are you sticking around?"

"Only until Radiology turns Trey loose."

While she waited, she impatiently checked the computer for his test results. One by one, the reports filtered in.

Normal chest film. No skull fracture. No concussion.

All she needed now was Dr. Abernathy's recommendation and she could grant Trey his wish. Of course, she could have granted it sooner if she hadn't gone overboard with the X-ray requests, but she wasn't going to risk overlooking *anything*. There would be hell to pay if she did, not only from her boss and Trey's, too, but also from Trey's adoring public.

Finally, an X-ray technician wheeled him into the trauma room. His normally relaxed mouth was pinched with apparent pain and the orbit of his other eye was slowly turning dark.

"What do you know," she said cheerfully. "Your eyes match."

He looked so forlorn she wanted to give him a hug. Now, *that* would cause the rumor mill to kick into gear…

"Great," he said glumly. "By the way, my CT scan was normal. Any chance I can have that ibuprofen now?"

Because she'd seen the report on her screen just moments ago, she agreed. "Absolutely."

While she doled out two pills, then two more when he glared at her, Nathan Abernathy rushed in, apologizing for his delay. Sierra looked on as he conducted his own exam, including the tests Trey had previously mentioned. A few minutes later, Roma waved to her from the doorway.

Sierra slipped outside the room. "What's up?"

"Dr. Donovan has a visitor."

"Only one?" she asked wryly.

Roma smiled. "Only one."

"Female, I'm presuming?"

"Yes, but—"

"She'll have to wait until Abernathy is finished."

"It would be better if she didn't."

"Ah, I get it. A VIP?"

"Dr. Donovan would think so."

How typical, Sierra thought with some disgust. *He's busy flirting with every woman he meets, but he has a girlfriend—a very important girlfriend—waiting in the wings.*

"I think you should talk to her before she sees him," Roma continued. "Prepare her for what he looks like."

Imagining a blonde bimbo falling apart and weeping over him because he wouldn't be able to take her dancing for a few weeks, Sierra grimaced. She glanced inside the trauma room and saw Abernathy continuing his joint manipulation. "Okay. Where is she?"

Roma pointed toward the nurses' station. "There."

Sierra glanced down the hall and saw a young girl fidgeting, her arms crossed in a self-protective gesture. As she turned, Sierra recognized her immediately.

Trey's VIP was the child from the labyrinth.

"Why...that's Hannah!" Sierra exclaimed.

Roma nodded, her eyebrows raised in question. "You know her?"

"I met her today in the garden. She talked about her uncle, but she didn't mention any names."

"Yeah, well, she's his niece." Roma's eyes filled with curiosity. "Who were you expecting?"

"No one in particular," Sierra muttered, too embarrassed to explain. "I got the impression young Hannah spends a lot of time here at the hospital."

"Some," Roma admitted. "During the summer months when school is out of session, she plays with the little ones in the hospital's day care. Dr. Donovan has worked out a deal where she gets 'paid' for helping because she's technically too old to be taking up a slot. Still, the arrangement works out for them and she's allowed to visit selected areas of the hospital. Frankly, I'm surprised she didn't spend the afternoon in our lounge, watching television."

"Then Trey…er…Dr. Donovan is her guardian?"

"Not officially. Hannah's dad travels a lot with his job and when he does, Hannah stays with Dr. Donovan."

"She doesn't have any other family? A grandmother, an aunt?"

Roma shook her head. "Their mom—Hannah's grandmother—lives in Arizona, so she isn't here, and neither is the older brother. He's a reporter, living in the Middle East, which leaves Trey and his brother. For the last few years Trey has practically raised that child."

Being a surrogate dad was a side of Trey that Sierra hadn't expected and, in fact, would never, *ever,* have imagined.

Ashamed because she'd immediately assumed the worst and not given him the benefit of the doubt, she glanced into the trauma room once again.

Trey's white face and the sheen above his upper lip indicated Nathan's manipulation wasn't particularly pleasant. If Hannah saw him looking so terrible, she wouldn't be reassured that her uncle wouldn't go the way of her mother.

"I'll talk to her," Sierra said. "By the time we're done, Abernathy should be finished with his exam."

Roma nodded. "If you don't need me for anything else, I'm clocking out. My hubby is barbecuing tonight and if I'm not there to supervise, he'll set the yard on fire."

"You're kidding, right?"

"I wish I was," the nurse finished glumly. "See you tomorrow."

As Sierra headed toward the nurses' station, Hannah looked in her direction. Recognition dawned, then a combination of fear and hopefulness that Sierra found painful to watch. Slowly, the girl took a step forward. Then another. And before Sierra knew it, Hannah was clutching her lab coat's sleeve.

"How is he? Mrs. Jones in the coffee shop said Uncle Trey had been beaten up. Is he gonna be okay? How sick is he? Is he...? Is he...?" Her lower lip quivered. "Will he be able to go home? If he has to stay the night, can I stay with him?"

Sierra hugged her, feeling the girl's shoulder shake. She also noticed something else...something that wasn't quite right...but she didn't have time to pursue that thought. "Your uncle wasn't beaten up."

"But Mrs. Jones—"

"Mrs. Jones was partially right. Two patients were fighting and your uncle didn't want any of us to get hurt, so he tried to separate them. The next thing we knew, he ended up in the middle and took a few punches. But he'll be okay," she hastened to add.

"Are you sure?"

"Absolutely," Sierra said. "I wouldn't lie to you."

The worried wrinkle on Hannah's forehead lessened. "He kept other people from getting hurt?"

She was glad she hadn't mentioned how she'd been the only one nearby. Who knew what story Hannah would tell and what conclusions others might draw if that piece of information became common knowledge. She didn't want gossip to say he'd been protecting *her*.

"Yes, he did."

"Then he was a hero," Hannah decided.

"No question about it," Sierra said cheerfully. "Would you like to see him now?"

Hannah's head bobbed so hard, her ponytail bounced. "Yes, please."

"Okay, but I have to warn you. He looks terrible." There was no sense in lying to the child. "But the bruises will fade and everything else will heal."

"He really looks bad?"

"I've seen far worse injuries," Sierra told her, "but to you, he might look pretty scary."

"But he will get better." Hannah stared at her intently, as if wanting to make sure Sierra wasn't simply telling her what she wanted to hear.

"He will," Sierra assured her. "Remember that when you see him. Until then, he'll need lots of help from you because with his hurt knee he won't be as mobile as he was."

Hannah nodded. "Okay." She squared her thin shoulders. "Can I go to him now?"

"Sure."

The girl walked beside her with determination on her face and in her step, but seconds before they reached the doorway, she slid her hand into Sierra's. Clearly, she wasn't as confident as she tried to appear.

Sierra hugged her again. "He'll be fine," she repeated. "No matter how frightening he looks, keep telling yourself that."

"Okay."

Sierra strolled into Trey's room to find Nathan standing off to the side while the two physicians talked. The sheen on Trey's upper lip and forehead had disappeared and although his face still showed signs of his discomfort, his expression was far less pained than before. The medication and the ice packs were obviously helping.

"Guess who I found in the hallway!" she exclaimed as she ushered Hannah inside.

A gasp came out of Hannah's mouth. Her eyes grew huge and her voice wobbled. "Uncle Trey?"

"Hi, sunshine," he said, holding out one arm. "I need a hug right now."

As Hannah uncertainly took a step forward, she glanced up at Sierra. "Is it okay?" she asked in a fearful little voice. "I won't hurt him, will I?"

Sierra smiled. "It's okay," she reassured her.

"I won't feel better until you do," he coaxed.

Immediately, Hannah dived into his embrace with such enthusiasm that Sierra winced from witnessing it. No doubt Trey had felt the jostle, but if he did, he hid his aches well throughout what was plainly a tender moment between the two.

The image of a battered Trey tightly hugging his niece would be forever seared into her brain. For all his similarities to David, this was one startling difference. His affection for young Hannah was obviously sincere, not feigned, and not given at his own convenience.

His niece obviously adored him as well because she sniffled and wiped her nose on Trey's scrub shirt.

"Hey," he said softly. "What's this? Tears?"

"No," Hannah denied unconvincingly as she stepped back, her hand still in his. "I was so worried about you, Uncle Trey. When I heard you got beaten up and they wouldn't let me see you or tell me how you were doing, I got so scared."

He glared at Sierra over Hannah's head. "They wouldn't let you see me?" he asked in the same mild tone that physicians had perfected—the same tone that didn't bode well for the person on the receiving end.

Sierra shrugged, ready to explain that she hadn't even *known* he had a niece until a few minutes ago, but Hannah beat her to it.

"They said you were in X-Ray. You were there for a *very* long time," she chided. "I had to wait and wait and *wait* until Dr. McAllaster found me. She told me everything that happened and how you are a hero."

His gaze still focused on Sierra, he raised an eyebrow. "A hero, eh?"

Hannah nodded briskly. "Oh, yes. You saw those two guys

fighting and tried to get them to stop before they hurt anyone else. I hope those guys went to *jail!*"

"They did," Sierra assured her, "but not before they asked me to convey their apologies to your uncle."

"That's a first," he remarked.

"You have Ben and Lamont to thank," she told him. "If those men ever come back, they'll definitely be on their best behavior, or they'll suffer the consequences."

One corner of his mouth turned up. "They must have really been intimidating."

"Yeah, well, their threat didn't sound too pleasant to me."

Hannah tugged on Sierra's arm. "Can we go now?" she asked plaintively. "Or do we have to stay longer?"

"That depends on what Dr. Abernathy says." Sierra glanced at the orthopedic specialist.

"We can turn him loose," Nathan said. "As far as I can tell, he's only stretched a few ligaments that aren't used to being stretched." He faced Trey. "For the next few days use ice, ibuprofen and elevate your leg. We'll wrap your knee to help with the swelling and keep it immobilized. When you're up and around—and I expect you will be when you feel more like yourself—" he grinned "—use crutches."

"Crutches?" Trey asked.

"Or a wheelchair. Take your pick. Oh, and no driving either."

"For how long?" Trey demanded.

"Until you can bend your knee without pain. I suspect a few days will be enough. If you aren't better in a week or so, we'll take another look."

Nathan's pager went off and he glanced at the display. "I'm off to the races again, I see. Anyway, if something dire happens, you have my number."

As soon as Nathan left, Sierra noticed Trey's downturned mouth. "What's wrong? He gave you good news."

Trey stared at her as if she'd grown a third arm. "Being

told to use crutches is *not* good news. It's overkill, if you ask me."

"Ah, but we didn't ask you," she said smugly. "We asked an *orthopedic* specialist."

"Uncle Trey?" Hannah interrupted. "If you can't drive, how are we going to get home?"

He stroked her hair. "That does present a bit of a problem, doesn't it? Not to worry, though. We'll ask someone for a ride."

"Who?" Hannah demanded as her eyebrows wrinkled.

"Roma won't mind," he assured her.

"She's gone home for the day," Sierra supplied. "Something about her husband barbecuing."

"Then Lamont or Ben—"

"They've left, too. Surely you know someone outside the hospital you can call. One of your old girlfriends, perhaps?"

This time, he glowered at her. "No."

She'd obviously poked a nerve, which didn't make sense. But the longer he took to think of a name, the deeper Hannah's worried wrinkle became. An idea began to form in Sierra's head.

"Hannah and I have one more option," he said slowly.

Knowing how he was a man used to getting his way, she anticipated his plan and shook her head. "No, you cannot drive yourself. I can't believe you'd endanger Hannah—"

"Who said anything about driving myself?" he asked. "I was going to call a cab."

"But, Uncle Trey," Hannah protested, "who'll help you up the stairs?"

"I'll manage, sweetie. Not to worry."

Obviously Hannah wasn't convinced because stark fear shone out of her eyes. And that fear convinced Sierra to speak up.

"I'd be happy to drive you," she offered lightly, seeing Hannah's face immediately light up. "The only problem is that my car's at home." Anticipating his question, she added, "I take the bus. It's cheaper and more convenient."

While it was definitely more cost-effective, she was stretching the truth to claim it was convenient. Invariably, no matter how hard she tried, she usually arrived at the hospital bus stop just after the bus had pulled away, forcing her to wait another fifteen to thirty minutes, depending on the time of day.

Then again, no one was waiting for her—not even a goldfish—so she'd learned to adjust.

"I couldn't impose."

Hannah's happiness faded before Sierra's eyes.

"It wouldn't be an imposition," she responded, well aware that if not for Hannah she would have been more than happy to send Trey home in a cab. "I'd be happy to be your chauffeur, if you don't mind waiting an hour or so for me to drive back."

"Please, Uncle Trey?" Hannah begged. "She said she wouldn't mind helping us."

Sierra watched as Trey clearly weighed his options. "I know, but it would be so much easier if we called a cab."

"No, it wouldn't. The seats are uncomfortable and the cars always smell funny." She wrinkled her nose. "We'd have to wait for one anyway, so we could just wait for Dr. McAllaster."

"If Hannah is tired of hanging around the hospital—" Sierra was already planning the logistics of her mission "—she can come with me while I run home. You can rest until we get back."

"Not fair. You two are ganging up on me," he protested.

"I wouldn't say that," Sierra said as she winked at Hannah. "We're only offering the most logical suggestion."

"The *most* logical is for you to take us home in my own car." He spoke to Hannah. "Go with Dr. McAllaster and fish my keys out of my locker. You know the combination."

Sierra listened in shock. "You want me to drive *your* car?"

"Sure. Why not? It'll save time for both of us."

His plan was sensible, even if it didn't address the details of how she'd find her own way home. However, that wasn't an insurmountable issue and could be resolved easily enough. She only hoped he lived within walking distance of a bus stop because she didn't have enough cash in her pocket for a cab and asking for money was out of the question.

"Do you have a place to park my vehicle at your house?" he asked.

"You want me to keep it?" she said.

"Why not? I won't be driving. This way, you can pick me up in the morning for work."

"Your car will be safe in the driveway behind my house, but I can't believe you want to see patients tomorrow."

"Being on crutches doesn't preclude me from treating people, so why shouldn't I report for duty?"

"Why not?" she sputtered. "You should be at home, resting. Do you really want to explain your two black eyes and banged-up leg to everyone who comes in? What sort of confidence will we instill in our patients if their doctor looks worse than they do?"

"Okay, fine. I can always hide in the office and take care of paperwork."

"Paper-pushing can't wait a day or two?"

"I have two very important meetings scheduled for tomorrow."

Sensing he wouldn't relent, she gave in. "Okay, fine. You're the boss. Come on, Hannah. Let's find your uncle's car keys."

After first making arrangements for Trey to borrow a set of crutches from the physical-therapy department, she and Hannah went to the staff lounge. Watching her open Trey's locker was a little unsettling, as if she, Sierra, were imposing on his personal space, but it had to be done.

The space inside was tidy—an obvious reflection of the man—and held only the bare necessities. An extra pair of scrubs hung on the hanger rod beside three starched, white lab coats with his name embroidered in black over the right breast pocket. A set of street clothes—chinos and a button-down, short-sleeved cotton shirt—dangled off another hanger. A shaving kit rested on the top shelf and a duffle bag rested on the floor.

Hannah ran one hand on the shelf behind the leather kit. "Here they are," she crowed triumphantly, holding them up for view.

"Great. Do you know where he parked?"

"Not exactly. He came in really, really early today. I had dance lessons this morning, so after my friend and I were finished with our class, her mom brought me here. I didn't see Uncle Trey until lunchtime."

So Hannah had been his date. How interesting.

Sierra stripped off her lab coat and tossed it into the hospital laundry bin before grabbing her purse out of her own locker. "No problem. Your uncle can tell us where he parked."

"Section two, row J. You'll see the logos of the local football and baseball teams in the back window," he replied when asked a few minutes later.

"Okay, I'll be right back," she said. "Hannah, can you ask someone to wheel your uncle to the side emergency entrance in about ten minutes?"

"We'll be there," the girl promised.

Sierra located his car without any trouble. The leather seats were hot, but she found two towels in the trunk to use as covers. Guessing the vehicle was Trey's pride and joy from the freshly waxed exterior and the spotless interior, she carefully maneuvered it through the parking aisles and gently braked to a stop in front of the ambulatory entrance.

As she rounded the car to greet her two passengers, she met two frowning faces instead of smiling ones. Her heart sank as she imagined the worst. Maybe Trey had changed his mind about accepting her help. Maybe he'd argued with Hannah. More likely, he'd refused a wheelchair ride to the door and Hannah had scolded him like the mother hen she seemed to be.

The man simply didn't understand the child's fears were rooted in losing someone important to her.

"Okay, you two," she said sternly. "What happened while I was gone?"

CHAPTER FOUR

"NOTHING," Trey ground out. "Can we just get in the car and go?"

"He fell," Hannah supplied as she climbed into the back-seat.

Sierra froze. "Oh, my gosh. Are you hurt?"

"I'm fine." He hobbled forward, flung open the passenger door then maneuvered himself inside.

Sierra wedged the aluminum crutches into the trunk then slid behind the wheel. Before she started the engine, she glanced at Hannah in her rearview mirror. "Is he fine, or do I need to haul him back inside?"

"I think he's okay," Hannah said importantly. "But it was close."

"How close?"

"Not close at all," Trey snapped. "The rubber grip on my crutch got caught in the rug and I stumbled."

Sierra had already guessed at the chain of events. "You refused a wheelchair, didn't you?"

"Everyone was busy and I'm quite capable of walking on my own," he grumbled.

"Yeah, I can see that," she answered wryly. "How far did you fall?"

"I did not fall. I *stumbled* and banged myself against the wall. Only my hip and my ego are bruised."

"Both will recover," she said cheerfully as she pulled into the traffic. "You can stop worrying, Hannah."

"Oh, but that's not the real problem, is it, Hannah?" he stated. "You may as well tell her the *full* story."

A quick glance showed Hannah with a tight-lipped expression on her face. "Hannah?" she coaxed.

"I don't know why he's making such a fuss about me," she complained as she stared out her window. "He's the one who's hurt."

Trey sighed. "Hannah was invited to a birthday party tonight—"

"And he's making me *go*," she wailed.

Sierra peeked at Hannah again to ask the obvious. "You don't want to?"

"I do, but—"

"It's for your best friend," Trey reminded her. "You've been waiting for this night for weeks. You were going to make jewelry, remember?"

"I changed my mind."

"Why?"

"Because you need me."

"Aw, Hannah—" he began.

"If I go," Hannah burst in, "who'll stay at home to take care of you?"

"I'll be fine by myself for a few hours."

"But what if you're not? You fell just walking down the hallway."

"I didn't fall. I tripped. No harm done."

"Yeah, but at home, something terrible could happen," Hannah informed him in a voice that sounded older than her years. "You could fall down the steps and not be able to get up. Or, worse, you could hurt your other knee."

"I promise I won't move from the sofa."

"I can't take the risk." Hannah crossed her arms as if her decision was final.

Trey rubbed his face then grimaced as if he'd rediscovered the painful areas he'd momentarily forgotten. "Hannah, sweetie, there's nothing to risk. I'll be fine at home by myself. I'll keep the phone with me at all times and if anything happens—anything at all—Tiffany's dad can bring you home right away."

"It doesn't matter, because I'm not going."

He let out a deep sigh before he met Sierra's gaze and shrugged helplessly.

Sierra understood the little girl's reasoning. After losing her mother and having a father who sounded as if he was absent more than he was present, the poor thing probably was racked with insecurities they couldn't begin to imagine. However, Sierra hated for her to give up something she'd obviously been anticipating for weeks because of an irrational fear. Clearly, Trey felt the same way. Unfortunately, he wasn't in a position to do anything about it. She was.

"Would you feel better if I stayed with your uncle to babysit? Only until your party ended, of course," Sierra offered, wondering if she'd completely lost her mind at some point during the day. Actually, that wasn't the case. She was only doing this for Hannah because it felt good to do something for a child who'd suffered too much tragedy already in her life. "That way, you can have fun instead of worrying if he'll do something stupid to hurt himself."

She met his startled gaze and winked. Slowly, he nodded and his eyes registered gratitude. "Now that sounds like an idea," he said enthusiastically. "What do you think, sunshine? Would you trust Sierra to look after me?"

Hannah scooted to the edge of her seat. "Would you? I promise I won't stay long—just until we make our necklaces. I won't even stay for cake and ice cream."

"Oh, cake and ice cream is a must," Sierra insisted. "You don't want to hurt your best friend's feelings by leaving early, do you?"

"Hannah, buckle up while we're driving," Trey interrupted firmly.

The little girl slid back and the click of the seat belt confirmed she'd obeyed. "Yeah, I wouldn't want to hurt Tiffie's feelings, but are you sure you don't mind, Dr. McAllaster? The party's supposed to start at six—we're having grilled hot dogs—so you'll have to make Uncle Trey's dinner for him."

"Dinner. Check."

"I'm not completely helpless," he protested.

Hannah ignored him. "I put today's newspaper beside his chair and I fixed a fresh pitcher of lemonade for him before I left for class this morning. Oh, and he can't have coffee after dinner because then he can't sleep."

She met Trey's gaze, noticing he was half amused and half embarrassed by his niece's "babysitting" list. "Newspaper, check. Lemonade, check. No coffee, check. Anything else?"

"Not that I can think of. But you can always call me. I'm speed-dial three on his phone."

"Speed-dial three," Sierra repeated. "I won't forget."

"The party ends at ten. If that's too late for you to drive home, maybe you could stay overnight at Uncle Trey's house."

Stay overnight? Not a chance!

"A sleepover is definitely out," Sierra said firmly. "Ten o'clock won't be too late for me to go home."

"You're sure you don't mind?" Hannah asked again, anxiously.

"I'm positive. You have a good time and don't worry about a thing," Sierra reassured her. "I'll look after your uncle."

"And you'll call me if you have a problem?"

Sierra wondered what Hannah thought she could do as a ten-year-old if Trey truly had a medical emergency, but she supposed it was part of the girl's need to be in control and avoid unwelcome surprises. "Scout's honor."

Suddenly, with that burden apparently lifted, Hannah's natural exuberance began to shine. "Tiffie's house is on the way to ours, but it's almost six now and I have to go home to get my gift first. Is that okay?"

"It's okay," she assured her. "The McAllaster Taxi Company is at your service."

Sierra followed Trey's directions until they pulled up in

front of a large brownstone. As soon as Hannah hopped out of the car to run inside for Tiffany's present, Trey let out a sigh. "Thanks for convincing her to go to the party. Sometimes Hannah forgets to be a ten-year-old."

"She does seem rather responsible for a girl her age."

"Unfortunately, with her mother dying so young, Hannah's grown up far too fast. My brother still hasn't gotten his act together and it's nearly been three years. I help out as much as I can so she'll have as normal a childhood as possible under the circumstances, but there are days when I feel like I'm fighting a losing battle."

"She loves you," Sierra said simply. "Watching out for you is natural to her."

"Yeah, well, thanks for giving her this night. She's been talking about it for weeks and I couldn't live with myself if she gave it up for me."

"Now she won't have to," she said lightly.

Hannah popped open the car door and slid in, breathless from her jaunt. "I'm ready," she said. "Oh, this is going to be so much fun. Thanks, Dr. McAllaster."

"Please, you're my boss for the evening, so call me Sierra."

Hannah giggled, obviously amused by the notion of giving orders to an adult.

Thanks to Trey's directions, Sierra parked in front of Tiffany's house about five minutes later. After listening to another set of last-minute reminders, she echoed Trey's admonition to have a great time.

"Behave yourself," he added as Hannah leaned between the seats to kiss his cheek.

"You, too," Hannah told them before she ran up the walk to ring the bell.

The easy banter between the two spoke of the warm relationship Trey had with his niece. The whole idea seemed at odds with his playboy reputation, but knowing how much time the two spent together Sierra began to wonder if some of his perceived romantic exploits might be undeserved. Either way, Hannah was a fortunate little girl.

Trey had always found Hannah's habit of echoing his last-minute counsel humorous until he realized how it must have sounded to Sierra. While he definitely approved of the idea of misbehaving with his new babysitter, the potential problems were more than he wanted to handle.

"She didn't mean anything by her comment," he said instead.

Sierra's chuckle was soft and musical. "I know. She's a great kid."

"I think so, even if she's ten going on thirty-five. I imagine she was frantic when you met her this afternoon."

"To be honest, I'd met her earlier in the day. I'd walked the labyrinth during my lunch break and she joined me. We had a nice visit, so when your little incident came up, I was able to talk to her as a friend and not a complete stranger."

"Then you're the lady she talked about over lunch."

"And you're the uncle she mentioned."

"Afraid so."

"I was prepared to track you down and scold you for expecting a child to occupy herself for hours on end at a hospital."

"Why didn't you?"

"Hannah was careful not to share last names. I suspect she knew what I'd do."

Trey smiled, touched by his niece's protective streak. "Smart girl. For the record, though, you wouldn't have told me what I don't already know. Wandering around the hospital and doing odd jobs isn't what she needs, but what else can I do? She spends as much time with her friends' families as we can coordinate but she needs more stability. The poor kid never seems to have a routine."

"Roma mentioned something about Hannah being paid to play with the kids in the day care."

"I had to do something so as not to offend her independent sensibilities," he said wryly. "Our arrangement has worked out well, although it's costing me a fortune."

"Then *you're* paying her?"

"Yeah, but don't say a word. It's worth every penny because the job occupies her time and allows her to earn spending money, both under adult supervision."

"She told me all the places she's 'approved' to visit on her own."

"Yeah, we're constantly negotiating that list," he said wryly. "I added the garden this summer and I set enough conditions that she complains it isn't worth visiting. I suspect my requirements aren't stopping her, though."

"I would have to agree."

"Still, our arrangement only lasts for the summer. This fall, she'll ride the school bus and I'll get home shortly after she does, so she won't be a latchkey child for more than an hour or two."

As she turned down his street, he said, "Park in front of the house. I won't have as far to walk and it'll be easier for you when you leave."

As Trey laboriously made his way up the walk, Sierra hoped he'd realize that taking a day to rest might be a good idea. Using crutches wasn't as easy as it appeared.

Inside, he sank gratefully into his recliner. "There's no place like home."

"No, there isn't," she agreed, gazing around the room for a snapshot of the man behind the handsome face.

The living room was neat and clean, but definitely had a lived-in look. Newspapers were piled haphazardly on the coffee table and today's edition lay on top, as Hannah had promised. A large basket beside the sofa overflowed with magazines, and a coffee cup sat on the end table next to Trey's oversize recliner.

A few throw rugs covered the hardwood floors and the leather furniture was grouped in a cozy arrangement around the fireplace. An oil painting of a clipper ship on stormy seas hung above the mantel. It was a room designed to cater to masculine tastes, although a few feminine touches—frilly pink throw pillows, a Cinderella afghan and a pair of ballet shoes—were obviously courtesy of Hannah.

"Are you ready for lemonade?" she asked.

He struggled to rise. "Yeah. I'll show you around."

"I can find the kitchen on my own."

"I know what you promised Hannah, but I don't need you to wait on me. Feel free to leave at any time."

"Getting rid of me already?" she teased.

This time, he looked uncomfortable. "I don't want you to feel obligated to stay."

"A promise is a promise," she said firmly. "Knowing your niece, she has a nanny cam in her bag and can see everything we do."

He shuddered. "A scary thought. Okay, knock yourself out. Yell if you can't find anything."

Sierra wandered through the lower level and soon returned with two glasses of iced lemonade. "I saw chicken breasts in the refrigerator. Were you going to fix those for dinner?"

"I was, but—"

"How does a chicken stir-fry sound?"

"Fabulous, but I don't expect you to cook."

"That's why I'm offering."

"We could just order out."

"We could," she agreed, "but I know how long delivery takes. I can fix my recipe in half the time. Besides…" She grinned. "I'm hungry."

"Then be my guest. Do I have all the ingredients you need?"

"It's a fairly basic recipe and easily adaptable to whatever's on hand. What are you doing?" she asked as he rose and positioned his crutches under his arm.

"I'm going upstairs to change."

"Can you manage on your own? With the stairs?" she clarified.

"I don't have a choice," he said wryly. "I'm definitely not

sleeping on the couch and I'm not wearing these clothes for days on end."

"Yes, but—"

"Don't worry. I'm a big boy. I can handle a few stairs."

"Like you handled the hospital hallway?"

"Hey," he protested mildly, "I just hadn't gotten the hang of using these things, but I'm okay now."

Sierra wasn't as certain. Less than ten minutes ago she'd seen how slowly he'd taken the six porch stairs outside. Now he seemed determined to tackle an entire flight.

"I'll follow you," she began.

"Not necessary," he insisted. "I'll be careful. I always am."

"Ah. 'Being careful' explains how you ended up in this predicament."

"Okay, change 'always' to 'most of the time.'" He made shooing motions. "Go. I'll be fine. If I'm not down by dinner-time, you can fetch me."

"Deal."

Sierra waited quietly as he began his ascent, ready to race to his rescue if necessary. By the time he reached the landing halfway up, he paused to look over his shoulder and grinned at her.

"See, Ma?" he teased. "I made it this far, so you can stop hovering now."

Caught in the act, Sierra's face warmed. "Hovering? I'm only following my boss's instructions to the letter."

"Your boss also mentioned something about dinner," he reminded her.

"Okay, okay. I'm going." Although she wanted to tiptoe behind to watch him proceed on the next leg of his journey, she didn't. Instead, she returned to the kitchen and listened for tell-tale thumps from above as she rummaged through his cupboards in search of ingredients.

She didn't hear so much as a squeaky floorboard.

As she sliced the chicken and julienned the carrots, she wondered why he seemed so uncomfortable accepting her help. A man who thrived on female attention would be more than grateful, wouldn't he? Or was his reticence because he hated appearing weak?

Her latter theory was more plausible, she decided, but tonight his wishes didn't matter. Fulfilling her vow to Hannah was most important. Sierra didn't know what sort of female influence the girl had in her young life, but she intended to prove herself trustworthy. Why that was important, she didn't know, but it was.

She paused in midchop as she reflected on the irony of the day's events. She'd steered clear of men like Trey for a long time and yet on her first day in Emergency, her life had already become intricately entangled with his.

Trey paused on the threshold of the kitchen as he watched Sierra prepare dinner. She'd tied the Barbecue Chef apron Hannah had given him for his last birthday over her clothes, but what surprised him most was that she'd taken off her heels and panty hose and was puttering around his kitchen barefoot.

Oddly enough, she seemed to fit in his domain as if she belonged, and he relaxed for the first time since he'd arrived home. He probably wouldn't have felt this way if he'd suspected Sierra had an ulterior motive for being there, but he knew differently. If not for Hannah, she would have happily packed him into a cab and waved goodbye.

In spite of knowing her lack of interest was for the best, the idea pricked his male pride.

For a few minutes, he watched her and pretended that his world had righted itself. That no one outside the hospital depended on him. That he was free to pursue whatever relationship he wanted. That he could dream of a woman at his side who'd be there when he was old and gray. He wanted to believe Sierra might be the woman he'd hoped to find someday, when his life wasn't so snarled with other commitments.

Unfortunately, none of those daydreams were possible.

However, possible or not, Sierra was there now and nothing said he couldn't enjoy the moment while it lasted.

"Dinner smells delicious," he commented as he hobbled his way inside to sit on a bar stool.

"Thanks." Her face turned a becoming shade of pink, which suggested she wasn't accustomed to receiving compliments. "I see you made it downstairs in one piece."

"I did. I'd offer you a glass of wine—"

She raised her glass. "Lemonade is fine. Besides, Hannah will be crushed if we don't drink it."

His stomach growled, reminding him of how long ago lunch had been. "How soon until the food's ready?"

Her smile did funny things to his chest. "A few minutes, so make yourself comfortable and I'll dish up a plate. How hungry are you?"

"Starved."

"Great, because I made plenty. I have a hard time cooking for one or two."

He spent the next several minutes talking shop, but as soon as they sat down to eat, he focused on his meal.

"Do you always fix food like this?" he asked, marveling at how she'd taken such basic ingredients as noodles, chicken, carrots and green peppers and turned them into a tasty meal.

"I used to," she admitted. "This isn't a dish I prepare for myself. I'd have leftovers for a week."

"I'll take your leftovers anytime," he said as he plowed into his serving, then stopped to savor a taste he hadn't expected. "Pineapple?"

"I found a can in your pantry," she said. "I hope you hadn't saved it for another recipe."

"I honestly forgot it was there. You're full of surprises, aren't you?" he asked.

Her eyes took on a wary expression. "I could say the same about you."

He shook his head and grinned. "Don't be ridiculous. I'm an open book. You, on the other hand... Out of all the cities in the country, what made you choose Pittsburgh? Do you have family nearby?"

"Unfortunately, no. My parents have been gone since my med-school days. I have two sisters—one in Oregon and one in Colorado. Other than an elderly aunt who lives in New Mexico, my family ties are minimal."

"You didn't want to move closer to them?"

"They have their lives and I have mine," she said lightly. "After they married and moved across the country, it became difficult to stay connected. Which is why I envy what you're doing for your brother and Hannah. You could have walked away and let the two of them struggle on their own."

Admittedly, he could have, but even if he hadn't promised his sister-in-law, Marcy, to help Mitch however he could, he wouldn't have deserted his brother. With his parents and oldest brother so far away, Mitch and Hannah were all he had left.

"The three of you are lucky you have each other."

He hadn't considered his family relationship in terms of luck, but she was right. In spite of feeling inadequate for the tasks he'd taken on out of necessity, he was fortunate to have developed such a special bond with his niece.

"I guess so," he said slowly.

"As for Pittsburgh," she continued, "why not choose it? With it being rated online as the 'most livable city,' there's something to see and do all the time."

"You sound like a brochure for the Chamber of Commerce," he teased.

She chuckled. "I do, don't I?"

"Then you've already explored a lot? Seen a play, visited the Carnegie Museum of Art, taken in a baseball game?"

"Not yet," she said, "but the options are available and that's what's important."

"So what *have* you seen and done?" he pressed, intending to file away the information for future reference, although he wasn't quite sure why.

"Not much, I'm afraid," she said ruefully. "I've spent most

of my time working and when I wasn't at the hospital or the minor-emergency clinic, I was unpacking or finding my way around town."

He focused on three words. "The minor-emergency clinic?"

"I work there on my days off and every other Saturday. I have a few debts I'm trying to settle."

Trey began to add things up. She took the bus to save money, didn't go out, ate an apple for lunch and was working two jobs on a physician's salary. According to his math, she was probably in hock up to her pretty eyebrows. The question was, why? She didn't seem the type to spend money faster than she earned it.

"I'm sure I'll have time to explore before long."

"Probably," he said, "but I'm puzzled about something. With your E.R. experience, why didn't you apply for a spot in my department?"

She twirled some noodles on her fork, but didn't eat it. "I got tired of the adrenalin rush you Emergency types crave. After several years, I was ready to leave the hustle and bustle to the people who thrive on the excitement. The position as hospitalist was perfect for what I wanted, so I applied for that job instead."

"Yet you still ended up on my team."

She shrugged. "A temporary arrangement. A detour, if you will."

He decided to test the waters. "Maybe you'll like working with us so much, you'll choose to stay permanently."

"Not a chance," she said firmly.

He smiled. "I can be very persuasive."

"I've no doubt you'll try," she said, "but you'll be wasting your time."

He disagreed. Oh, he understood not everyone was cut out for Emergency and if that was her final decision, so be it. However, whether she changed her career plans or not, any time he spent with Sierra would not be wasted.

* * *

By the time Hannah arrived shortly after ten o'clock, the credits were rolling to Trey's action-adventure movie and he was fast asleep.

"Did you enjoy yourself?" Sierra whispered.

"Oh, yes," Hannah whispered back. "See the necklace we made? I used all my favorite colors."

Sierra dutifully admired the jewelry hanging around Hannah's neck as an unexpected pang of longing struck. If she'd had a daughter, she would be doing the same thing—welcoming her home after a party with her friends, being impressed by whatever craft project she'd proudly hauled home.

Sadly, she didn't have a daughter, and this moment with Hannah was a onetime event. Perhaps someday, when she felt as if she could trust a man again, she'd see her dream fulfilled. Until then, she wouldn't dwell on what she didn't have.

As she fingered the beads and accidentally touched Hannah's skin, Sierra noticed something else—her collarbone stood out rather prominently for a child her age. Her mental alarms clanged again, but if she was fortunate enough to spend more time with Hannah, she'd decide if she actually had cause to worry or if she was simply imagining what wasn't there.

"I'm glad you had a good time," she whispered.

Hannah smiled from ear to ear. "Oh, yes. Thank you so much for looking after Uncle Trey for me. How is he?"

"Doing well. He rested in his chair and dozed off halfway through the movie."

"I see."

Sierra followed Hannah's gaze. If anything, Trey's raccoon appearance had become more pronounced. His eyes were closed and a lock of hair had fallen endearingly over his forehead. One foot stuck out from under the Cinderella afghan Sierra had tossed over his bare legs when the room had grown chilly.

"This is great," Hannah enthused. "I'm going to take his

picture. For my scrapbook." With that, she whipped out her cell phone and snapped his photo from several angles.

Sierra wondered how he'd react when he saw himself. No doubt he'd be less than thrilled by the girly afghan covering his body, but in her opinion the pink fairy-tale design didn't detract from his masculinity at all.

"Should we wake him?" Hannah whispered after she'd finished her photo shoot.

"I think not."

Hannah nodded. "Yeah, he looks pretty comfortable where he is."

Then, because Sierra didn't know what the bedtime ritual for a ten-year-old girl was, she asked, "Need any help getting ready for bed? Reminders about brushing your teeth, washing your face and behind your ears?" She winked.

Hannah's eyes grew wide, as if Sierra's questioning was a new experience for her. "I can manage," she said, before her wonderment turned into shy delight. "Uncle Trey asks the same things, but his voice is deeper. You sound more like Tiffany's mom."

Sierra heard the wistful tone in Hannah's voice and her heart went out to the child. She wanted to stick around to tuck her into bed, but it wasn't her place. She settled for brushing a loose lock of hair out of Hannah's face.

"I appreciate that you think so. It means a lot," she said kindly. "Now, why don't you lock the door behind me and get ready for bed?"

Hannah nodded. "What time will you come by in the morning?"

"We'll let your uncle sleep in," Sierra decided. "He can use the extra rest."

"He won't be happy," she warned.

"Then he can call me to complain." Sierra switched off the television. "Now, off to bed, young lady."

As soon as she'd silenced the TV, Trey straightened in his chair. "Hey, I was watching that."

"You were sleeping," Sierra told him.

"You were," Hannah confirmed.

"I was resting my eyes," he protested.

"Of course," Sierra said, winking at Hannah. "Now that you're awake, you can go upstairs to bed."

"Good idea." He struggled to his feet and slipped his crutches under his arms. "About tomorrow…I'm taking a sick day."

Sierra studied him in surprise. "I thought you had two important meetings."

"They'll have to manage without me."

"Wow. What changed your mind?"

He grinned. "I saw myself in the mirror earlier."

Hannah giggled. "You do look pretty scary, Uncle Trey. You'll frighten your patients."

"I can't have that, now, can I?" he said. "Regardless, keep the car, Sierra, and when I'm ready to report back to work, you can return it."

"I wouldn't feel right—" she began.

"At least drive it home tonight," he said.

"The bus stop is—"

"Too far away to walk to by yourself in the dark," he said. "Please, take it. For my own peace of mind."

She told herself she was only accepting his offer so he wouldn't spend the night worrying instead of resting. It had nothing to do with the sheer joy of driving a well-tuned, late-model vehicle once again. Or the fact that she was guaranteed another visit when she could test her theory about Hannah.

"Okay. I'll keep your car overnight," she agreed. "After that, we'll see."

"Then you'll come back tomorrow to check on us?" Hannah asked, her expression hopeful.

Sierra glanced at Trey, who wore a speculative expression as he studied his niece. "I have to return your uncle's wheels," she said pointedly. "So, yes, I'll come back tomorrow."

Trey seemed hesitant at first, but then, as if he'd made a decision of some sort, he smiled at her. "Hannah and I will look forward to seeing you." He took two steps forward, but his crutch caught in a rug and he stumbled.

Immediately, Sierra braced herself to block his fall. A second later, one crutch clattered to the floor and her arms were wrapped around his waist.

For a long minute, she breathed in the pleasantly masculine scent she'd come to recognize. His mouth hovered dangerously close and she could almost feel his stubble-lined cheek. "Did you hurt anything?" she asked inanely.

"Only my pride. Again," he said ruefully, "but for this kind of save, I'll sacrifice it anytime."

"Down, Rover," she said softly. "We have an audience."

"More's the pity."

"Maybe you shouldn't tackle the stairs tonight," she said.

"Maybe not," he agreed, "but I'm going to."

"In that case, I'll follow you to the top."

"Hannah can—"

"You'll squash her like a bug if you fall," she warned, "so stop arguing."

He stopped.

"I'll turn on the lights upstairs so he can see where he's going," Hannah chirped.

Her offer broke the spell holding them together. As the ten-year-old bounded upstairs to flick on the light switches, Sierra noted his reluctance to release her. She half expected him to say something—*anything*—but he simply turned toward the stairs.

She followed, keeping one hand on his back to steady him. If he was irritated by her actions, he didn't complain. At the top of the stairs, outside his bedroom, he paused. "Would you like to help with my shower and tuck me into bed, too?"

She hadn't considered how he'd manage his personal needs. "I probably should—" she began.

"I was joking, Sierra. I can handle a shower by myself."

"Downstairs, you tripped over your own feet," she pointed out. "Do you honestly believe you're a match for a slippery shower? Or do you *want* a paramedic team to scrape you off the floor while you're wearing your birthday suit?"

"I appreciate your concern, but I'm taking a shower. Goodnight, Sierra."

She was ready to retrace her steps, but Hannah's look of sheer panic changed Sierra's plans. She couldn't leave now, any more than she could have performed neurosurgery.

"I'll say my goodnights after you're finished in the bathroom," she said briskly, noticing Hannah's resultant expression of relief. "So, hop to it, Harry. The night isn't getting any younger."

"I'll pick out your clothes, Uncle Trey." Hannah rushed into his room and began digging in his dresser drawers.

Sierra shooed him into his room. "And I'll sit here on the bed, ready to spring into action at a moment's notice." She was grateful his niece was rummaging through his underwear so she didn't have to.

With a disgusted grunt, he hobbled into his master bathroom and closed the door with a not-so-quiet click. A few seconds later, a muttered curse followed the metallic thump of a crutch hitting the tile floor.

Hannah winced. "I hope he's okay."

"He's fine. On the other hand, his crutches probably aren't."

"Do you think we hurt his feelings when we suggested he couldn't do things for himself?"

"No, honey. His pride is a little bruised, along with everything else, but he'll recover. Now, go on and get ready for bed."

Sierra listened to Trey's grunts behind the closed door and imagined his contortions as he undressed. If his lean leg had been a sight to drool over, his bare chest would probably take her breath away.

Heaven help her, but her hormones wanted desperately for him to take her breath away.

Finally, she heard the water running. Satisfied he'd gotten

that far in the process without a mishap, she lay back on his amazingly comfortable king-size bed.

The day had turned out so differently from how she'd imagined. Normally, she would have been in bed by eight-thirty in order to rise in time for her shift to begin at six. From the way tonight was turning out, it would be at least another hour before she fell asleep.

Late night or not, it had been a pleasant evening. Trey had asked the inevitable questions, but if he'd realized she'd glossed over some of her answers, he hadn't pressed her for more information. She wasn't ashamed of her past—at least, not most of it—but she didn't want to rehash every detail either.

Hannah was truly a lucky little girl, she decided as the sound of running water lulled her into a relaxed state. Her father may not be around much, but as far as she could tell Trey had stepped into the role quite well. He'd obviously do anything for that child.

She yawned, wondering when Hannah had last visited a doctor. She'd work on an opportunity to tactfully suggest a physical—Marissa would probably be willing. School was scheduled to start in a few weeks so maybe that would present a good excuse...

Her mind wandered as she compared Trey the charming playboy physician with Trey the honorary father whose sole focus was on his niece. Which one was real, which one was pretense?

She shifted positions and rolled into a low spot in the mattress. Obviously, she'd found Trey's favorite side of the bed. A fresh dose of his scent came from the pillows, making it remarkably easy to imagine him lying beside her.

"Some watchdog you are." His deep voice was filled with humor. "I'm slip-sliding around, struggling to stay upright, and you're in here, snoozing without a care in the world."

Startled by his unexpected presence, she bolted upright. "I was listening for you," she protested weakly, noticing his damp hair and a few water droplets clinging to his broad shoulders. The stubble on his face had disappeared, too, causing her to wonder how long she'd been in her half-awake state.

"Yeah, right." He glanced toward the doorway. "Is Hannah asleep?"

"If not, she soon will be."

He still hadn't moved. "Good. She's got to be tired. It was a busy day."

"For all of us," she agreed.

He propped his crutches against the wall. "Then, considering the furniture you're occupying, did you change your mind about sleeping over?"

CHAPTER FIVE

OVER the next few days, Trey still smiled whenever he thought about how Sierra had nearly mown him down in her haste to leave. If he'd needed proof that she wasn't interested in a romance, her actions would have provided it.

However, as the week had worn on, his resolve to remain uninvolved with a woman—especially Sierra—had wavered. He'd first planned to thank her politely for her assistance when she'd returned his car the next day, thereby ending their off-duty association. However, after lunch, Hannah had turned into a clock-watcher as she'd waited for Sierra's arrival. If not for her pleading puppy-dog expression, he wouldn't have invited Sierra to stay for dinner.

During that one meal between the three of them somehow he'd lost complete control of his life. Hannah had outlined an itinerary for the rest of the week that had been completely unexpected, not to mention impossible because of his no-driving directive. Shopping, errands, dentist appointments and even a movie with her friend Tiffany had suddenly and mysteriously filled their previously empty calendar.

On day three of his exile, the pain in his knee had disappeared to the point where he'd wanted to abandon his crutches and return to work, but his boss had encouraged him to use his accumulated personal leave until his face wasn't quite so colorful. He'd been ready to resume his place as family chauffeur and end Sierra's reason for visiting every night, but

Hannah had literally bloomed under his colleague's attention and he didn't have the heart to deny her Sierra's company.

He'd also caught his niece occasionally studying him with a fearful expression when they were alone, as if she expected him to keel over unexpectedly, so, to give her peace of mind, he'd held his tongue and allowed Sierra to stop by every evening to check on them.

And so, the subterfuge continued. Given his reluctance to rely on anyone—his family's problems and responsibilities were *his* to deal with—he had to admit that having Sierra around for conversation and companionship was…pleasant. And when his brother had called to announce he was delaying his return, Sierra had calmly defused Hannah's disappointment by pointing out how her uncle needed her for those few extra days, so perhaps it was a good thing she wasn't going home just yet.

He couldn't argue that Sierra had helped in ways he hadn't dreamed of or expected. The best part was that she never looked at him with a starry-eyed gaze or flirted mercilessly. She was the first woman in a long time—the first *available* woman, that was—who didn't respond to him like an adolescent groupie. He hadn't realized how wearisome those reactions had become until now.

Trey had also discovered how nice it was to default on certain responsibilities—braiding Hannah's unruly mane, and discussing whether a pink shirt looked better with brown, black or khaki shorts. He was already dreading the day when he'd have to buy feminine-hygiene products because he'd bet a week's salary that Mitch would be out of town for that event.

In any case, he'd begun to realize that he didn't want the week to end. Not because he felt less stressed than usual— which some might attribute more to his impromptu vacation than Sierra's presence—but because having Sierra in his life seemed better than a vacation itself.

It was strange, really. He'd always believed romantic involvements made one vulnerable—a concept learned from

Mitch, and now Sierra—which was why his affairs had never progressed beyond the casual sort. And yet he found himself wanting and wishing for the domestic bliss that so many of his colleagues enjoyed—the same domestic bliss he'd shunned. But how could he, when love didn't last—it usually didn't—and it was too difficult to pick up the pieces and go on?

And why had Sierra triggered those feelings? Had her ability to relate to his family's losses like no one else been the cause? Maybe it had happened because she was struggling to regain her footing, too, and the notion had aroused his protective instincts? Or could it be because she and Hannah had bonded so quickly and effortlessly, giving him a glimpse of a future if he only reached out and grabbed it?

The last question was most worrisome. While he'd like to get to know Sierra better—maybe even enjoy a seduction—because they had a lot in common, he had to be careful no one suffered any heartbreak, on either side, when things didn't work out.

Now that he was back to work and Hannah at home with Mitch, maybe he should just ask Sierra to dinner, purely as a token of appreciation for everything she'd done for them. What came after that would depend on how their evening went.

He'd just left the lounge for a much-needed cup of coffee when Roma buzzed by and his phone chimed the arrival of a text message. "Gunshot victim's on his way," Roma called out before he could read the digital display. "ETA is three minutes."

Trey grabbed a yellow gown and a pair of goggles from a waiting cart without breaking his stride. "Who's available?"

"Dr. McAllaster. She's already in the bay."

He pulled the paper gown over his scrubs and fixed the clear shield over his face. Gunshots were always messy affairs. "Do we know anything else?"

"Thirty-five-year-old male. Paramedics think it was self-inflicted." She shook her head. "I hate those. One always has to ask if it was on purpose or by accident."

"Do the reasons matter?" he asked wryly. "We still have to try and undo the damage."

"So true."

Out on the dock, he glanced over the assembled team. Roma, himself, two more nurses and Sierra, who didn't quite look like herself. Her face was white, her mouth pressed into a hard line, and her hands were folded protectively across her chest.

"Are you okay?" he asked her in low voice.

"Yeah, sure. I'm fine. Why wouldn't I be?"

The ambulance rounded the corner and began to reverse toward them. "Is everybody ready?" Trey asked.

Heads nodded, but Sierra wanted to scream a heartfelt 'No.' No, she wasn't ready. There wasn't enough time left in the universe for her to be ready. A motor-vehicle accident, a stabbing, a heart attack, yes, but a gunshot wound? No. Absolutely not.

Her stomach churned as the emergency vehicle rolled to a stop and Trey stepped forward to yank open the door. Knowing there were plenty of waiting hands to pull out the stretcher, she hung in the background and used those few extra minutes to swallow her nausea.

As soon as the paramedic locked the wheels in place with a snap, Sierra braced herself to glance at the victim.

She was prepared for the sight of blood, but the head of dark curly hair, the lanky frame, the tailored suit and expensive wingtips flashed her into the past....

"BP is one-ten over sixty and falling. No lung sounds on the right side."

"Small entrance wound near his heart. Large exit wound on his upper back. Call a thoracic surgeon and get six units of O-neg blood in him stat!"

"He's bleeding out."

"BP is falling."

"Where's that blood?"

This is *not* David, she reminded herself. *This is not David.* It's someone else. Someone who looks like him. Someone who's a complete stranger. She could be objective... She *would* be objective.

"Sierra! Help me find and plug the leak," Trey ordered.

The sound of her name catapulted her into the present. She'd obviously been doing the right things with the still-functioning part of her brain because, unlike the case that had convinced her to voluntarily relinquish her previous ED position, she wasn't huddled at the foot of the gurney, gaping like a medical student at his first trauma. She stood on the opposite side of the bed across from Trey in the trauma room and in the middle of the action.

"Sierra? Are you with me?" His dark eyes pinned her as effectively as an X-ray film to a viewing box.

She shook off her thoughts and squared her shoulders. "Yeah."

He spoke to no one in particular. "Someone, take over his airway. Get me blood gases, a stat H and H, and six units of O-neg brought here now. From the way the blood is running, I think he's nicked his aorta. We're going to have to cross-clamp it. Let's get these clothes off."

Sierra cut through the man's sleeves, careful to avoid any already-created holes so as not to destroy any police evidence. Out of the corner of her eye, she saw someone else remove his shoes and trousers and place the clothing in a bag. As soon as she'd helped clear the field for Trey, she prepared to assist in opening the man's chest.

"Hemoglobin is four point nine," a nurse reported.

"I'm almost surprised it's that high," he muttered as she saturated the patient's skin with povidone-iodine to cleanse it while another nurse hung two units of blood. Seconds later, a sterile drape covered the area and he said one word.

"Scalpel."

Sierra watched as he sliced open the man's chest. Anticipating his request, she handed him a rib spreader.

"Oh, man," he said as he revealed a lung that was nothing more than a lump of tissue. "This guy's a mess."

The pericardial sac had been ripped open and bright red blood squirted like a geyser. "Clamp!" he ordered.

Sierra's gloved hands were slippery with blood as she passed sterile towels and more clamps while another nurse suctioned. Finally, the bleeding slowed and the two bags of O-negative were already empty.

"Hang two more," Trey ordered.

Walter Rains, a sixty-year-old cardiovascular surgeon, peeked over their shoulders. "Status?" he barked. As soon as Trey finished his report, Walter nodded. "We'll take it from here."

A fresh team arrived to wheel the patient to the elevators and the drama for the emergency staff was over. Although no one said a word, there was a collective sigh of relief because their patient hadn't cashed out during their watch. The outcome now rested in the surgeon's hands.

As after most traumas, the room was a mess. The nursing staff began to tidy it for future use while they chatted, but Sierra didn't join in their conversation. She simply stripped off her gloves and tossed them in the trash can before pulling off and wadding up her gown to follow.

Tamping down her nausea at the metallic smell of blood permeating the room, she scrubbed her hands and arms then scrubbed again, taking as much care as a surgeon about to operate.

"Can everyone give us a minute?" Trey asked mildly as he joined her at the sink.

Sierra noticed how the staff exchanged puzzled glances then slipped out. Only Trey remained.

Instinctively, she knew what was coming. She'd hoped he hadn't noticed her inattention, but apparently not. She braced herself for the inevitable questioning, which began as soon as the room cleared.

"Are you okay?" he asked.

She decided to bluff her way through, although she didn't

hold much hope for success. Charming or not, Trey Donovan possessed a tenacious streak. "Of course. We got our patient to the O.R. without dying, so why wouldn't I be?"

"I don't know. For a few seconds I thought you'd checked out."

Then he *had* noticed how part of her mind had been miles away.

"I, uh…"

"You what?" he prompted.

If he'd been observant enough to notice, she wouldn't be able to play down her actions. She knew it and she knew that he knew it, too. "For a few seconds, he reminded me of another case. Haven't *you* ever encountered a situation you'd experienced before?"

"We all have, but you froze."

"I did not," she denied. "I knew what was happening all of the time. Maybe it took me two extra seconds to jump for you—and if you want to accuse me of freezing, it's your prerogative—but I. Did. My. Job."

Her ground-out words hung in the air. "You did," he agreed, "but I need you. All of you, all the time. Not after a five-second delay."

She hated being reminded of her lapse. More importantly, she hated that after all these months, her response was still lacking for a doctor with her experience.

"It won't happen again." She twisted the taps and yanked several paper towels out of the holder to dry her hands. Before she could storm out, he said her name in a softer, gentler tone—a tone that caused her throat to clog with tears of sadness, guilt and frustration. It was the kind voice that drilled through her defenses more quickly and more effectively than if he'd continued his harangue.

She swallowed hard. "What?" she asked dully.

"Who did this patient remind you of?"

Slowly, she faced him. His expression was impassive, but his eyes suggested he'd already guessed the answer. He was only waiting for her to confirm his suspicions.

She squared her shoulders and met his gaze without flinching. "My husband."

He nodded slowly. "I thought so. I'm sorry."

Then, because suddenly the air in the room seemed to disappear and she couldn't breathe, she turned on one sneaker and headed outside to the labyrinth where she felt at home with everyone else who hoped to find solace there.

She was striding along the circular path, her eyes shielded from the sun with dark glasses, her head down, when he fell into step beside her. "Tell me about that day," he said.

She didn't answer for a few turns because she didn't quite know how to begin, but she'd heard the hint of an order in his voice, so she chose her starting point.

"We were a trauma center and ambulances brought us patients in a steady stream all day long, every day," she said. "We hardly had time to clean up after one before another arrived. Everyone who came was critical, all needing instant decisions, instant treatment. Hurry, hurry, hurry. You know the drill."

He nodded.

"Some days, I never saw a patient's face. I was so busy treating the stab wounds, the gunshots, the lacerations, the ruptured spleens and everything else you can name, that I only had a vague impression of the individual. Large, small, young or old, it didn't matter. If I took time to see the person for who he or she was, it was time the patient often couldn't afford."

She drew a deep breath and tried to recite the events objectively. "One day, a man came in with a gunshot wound, just like today. I tried to stop the bleeding, but nothing I did was effective. I'd called for a surgeon, but he was slow getting there. For some reason, and I'll never understand why other than perhaps it was fate, I glanced at the man's face and recognized him. It was David."

The shock had been paralyzing, then fear and dread had taken hold. Fear that she couldn't save him and dread that she couldn't keep him alive until someone with more skill could step in and do the impossible. For all of his faults and all of their personal problems, she hadn't wanted him to end their marriage on such a cowardly note.

"Then what?"

"As soon as I recovered from the shock that I'd been working on my own husband, I was more determined than ever to save him. His vitals were horrible and when he flatlined, I kept going. I look back and see that I acted like a madwoman, ordering one drug then one procedure after another. The staff kept telling me he was gone, but I wouldn't listen. Finally the surgeon we'd called in literally pulled me away from the table, grabbed my hands and called an end to the code we'd called. I would have worked on David indefinitely if Dr. Barnes hadn't intervened."

"You did everything you could."

She'd told herself the same thing on countless occasions, especially whenever a fresh wave of guilt had struck her. She'd replayed every minute and analyzed every order until she'd thought she'd go crazy.

"I like to think I did," she said slowly, "but his family accused me of incompetence. Our marriage had been in trouble for years—in fact, the only good times we had together were in the first twelve months—and they believed I'd purposely let him die. It wasn't true, of course, and the staff who worked with me all told them so, but in the end there was an investigation. I was exonerated, but not before they vilified me to the point where I doubted every decision I made."

"So you left the E.R.?"

She nodded, remembering how she'd felt like a failure. "Eventually. I'd wanted to stick it out because I loved working in Emergency, but the constant barrage of cases like his took its toll. The stress became more than I could handle. When I decided I was more of a hindrance than a help, I begged for a transfer."

"You had PTSD," he stated.

"So my therapist said," she answered wryly. "Fortunately, once I accepted that I truly *had* done everything I could—that his injuries had been fatal regardless of which doctor had treated him—I was able to move past the incident and function as usual."

"Until our patient today brought back all those negative feelings."

"From his curly black hair down to his expensive shoes," she admitted wryly. "His case was so much like David's, it was uncanny."

"Thanks to me dragging you back into Emergency, you had a flashback."

She heard the disgust in his voice and hated that he'd assumed responsibility for her lapse. "It only lasted for an instant," she corrected. "And it wasn't your fault. We don't have any control over the cases we receive."

"No, but you were nervous before you saw him," he pointed out.

She'd tried so hard to defuse her anxiety but had obviously failed if Trey had noticed. "Under the circumstances, is it any wonder why gunshot injuries aren't my most favorite condition to treat?"

After hearing her story, Trey felt guilty for making her relive such a traumatic event. No wonder she hadn't willingly given up her position on the fifth floor. No wonder she'd vowed that nothing he said or did would convince her to stay in Emergency past her predetermined time limit.

"This is why you wanted a change," he mused aloud.

Her chuckle was humorless. "You can see how that's working out for me," she said wryly, her reference to her new assignment obvious.

"I'll talk to Dr. Keegan—"

"No, you won't," she declared. "I'll admit I didn't want to be here at first, but I won't quit. I need to prove to myself that I'm not a coward. That I *can* handle working in the ED, even if I prefer to work elsewhere."

"You're certain?"

"I agreed to sixty days and I have fifty-three left. Unless you're afraid I can't do my job…?"

As much as he hated to point out the obvious, he owed his patients the very best. "You said yourself a few seconds can make a difference for a successful outcome. What if you zone out again and you're the only doctor in the room?"

"I've handled traumas successfully before," she insisted. "What happened today won't happen again."

He hated to be the proverbial bad guy, but he'd learned one principle from his mentors. Pressure either strengthened an individual by causing them to dig deep inside for the guts to carry on, or it broke them.

Whether Sierra had hesitated or frozen, her lapse had only lasted for seconds. The truth was, he completely understood why she'd reacted as she had. If he'd been in a similar situation, he could easily have responded as she had, or worse. In fact, if he hadn't been watching her because he'd sensed she was as nervous as a doctor preparing to sit for a board exam, he would never have noticed.

Sierra had the right stuff inside her. He simply wanted her to believe she had it, too.

"How do you know?" he asked. "Are you one-hundred-percent certain you won't freeze again?"

She stopped in her tracks and pulled off her glasses to meet his gaze. "How do you know you'll keep your wits about you when a tough case comes in? That you won't be tired, or distracted by another situation so that it takes a few seconds to pull your thoughts together?"

"We're trained to be objective—to focus on the person in front of us and not let our personal feelings interfere."

"Exactly. Today was my first test since I accepted that David's outcome was beyond my control. I wish I'd earned an A, but I believe I came rather close. Don't kick me out of school on the basis of one exam."

"I'll give you the benefit of the doubt this time," he said, "but—"

"I know. If it happens again—and it won't—I'm gone. You won't have to make that decision," she tacked on.

"Okay. I trust you." While their patients were Trey's primary concern, Sierra on a bad day was still better than the alternative of a vacant position. Worse yet, he could end up with Dr. Madison or Dr. Warren.

Meanwhile, he intended to shore up her obviously shaky confidence while staying alert for potential problems. Fortunately, neither task posed a hardship.

"However," he added, "if you ever feel as if you can't handle a situation—emotionally or otherwise—I expect you to tell me."

Relief flashed in her eyes. "I will," she promised.

"Okay, then. We've settled that, so shall we go back to work before the staff think we've deserted them? Or before they speculate on why the two of us disappeared in the middle of our shift?"

A smile slowly appeared on her face. "We'd better," she agreed as she started toward the emergency door.

He matched his stride to hers. "First, though, I want to ask you to dinner."

A puzzled wrinkle appeared on her brow. "What for?"

"You helped Hannah and me so much last week, I owe you."

"You don't owe me a thing. I helped for no other reason than because I wanted to."

"Maybe, but I still want to pay you back in some way."

She suddenly smiled. "Don't tell me you're feeling guilty."

"Guilty? Why would I feel guilty?" he bluffed.

"Don't sound so innocent, Dr. D.," she teased. "You weren't nearly as helpless as you pretended to be."

He froze. "You knew?"

"By Thursday, I'd noticed you were bearing weight on your right leg and only used your crutches for show."

"You didn't say a word," he accused.

"It seemed best not to," she admitted. "After her dad called to say he wouldn't come home as soon as he'd planned, Hannah was obviously disappointed and felt rejected. I turned your pretense into her blessing because playing nurse gave her a sense of purpose and value. How could I rob her of feeling needed?"

His already-high opinion of Sierra soared. Any other woman of his acquaintance would have either been furious at the deception or ruined his whole plan. He couldn't think of anyone who would have played along and given priority to the emotional needs of his niece. Although... An unwelcome thought crossed his mind.

"You didn't have any other ulterior motive?" he asked.

For a fraction of a second, indecision flashed on her face before understanding appeared in her eyes. "Oh, I get it. You think I was only hanging around because of your witty personality and great body. Oh, and did I forget to mention your dazzling, *dramatic* profession as a physician?"

Her description, coupled with her completely unimpressed demeanor, made him realize how foolish—and how arrogant—he'd sounded. "You wouldn't be the first," he defended.

"Yeah, well, I've got better things to do than stroke your ego," she said without heat. "I'll leave that to the rest of your fan club."

She'd cut him down to size and he discovered he liked it. "Without a doubt, you are absolutely amazing, Sierra McAllaster."

She grinned. "Because I figured out your devious plot? Because I'm not one of your brainless bimbos?"

"All of the above and more," he answered. "So, are we on for dinner tonight?"

She nodded. "Yes."

Contrary to what Trey believed, Sierra had given her time the previous week for several reasons. His motherless niece had not only touched her heart, but her concerns about Hannah's health wouldn't fade.

Now that Hannah had gone home and Trey was back at work, she'd been wondering all day how to raise the subject. His dinner invitation gave her the perfect opportunity and she spent the rest of her shift mentally replaying the points she wanted to stress.

Fortunately, he'd suggested going immediately after work for a drink first, and she'd agreed.

Most hospitals had a wide assortment of eating establishments within walking distance for both staff and patients' convenience. Good Shepherd was no exception, although, from the conversations Sierra had overheard, Doc Whitby's was the place of choice at the end of a day because of their well-stocked bar and tasty grilled sandwiches.

Sierra walked into the restaurant with Trey at her side and immediately felt at home. Each dining area was enclosed by five-foot-tall walls, allowing the guests maximum privacy. The tables for large parties were surrounded by potted plants to also give the illusion of separation from other diners. Televisions dotted the walls so those who dropped by could catch up on the latest headline news during their meal, or stick around to watch an evening sports broadcast.

She followed the waitress to a booth in the corner, aware of the heads turning in her direction as they walked by. No doubt everyone was wondering just who Trey Donovan's companion was.

As soon as the girl took Sierra's order for a glass of white zinfandel and his request for a draft beer, Sierra couldn't hold back her curiosity.

"How did you get the name Trey? Did your parents name you after your dad and grandfather? Could you be John Donovan the Third?" she teased.

He laughed. "Nope. Trey is official. According to family folklore, I was the third child—the third boy, in fact—and my parents couldn't decide on a name. They had to choose something or they couldn't take me home from the hospital so because my dad loved to play card games, he told them Trey and it stuck."

"Having older brothers must have been nice."

"Up to a point," he admitted. "The oldest, Zach, always looked out for Mitch and me. He's a reporter and lives in

Israel right now. Next came Mitch, who's Hannah's dad. He's a pharmaceutical salesman and has a large territory, which is why he's rarely at home. Then there's me."

"Your parents?"

"My parents retired to Arizona to live near my mom's sister, who's in poor health. I try to fly out twice a year to visit."

"Do they see their granddaughter often?"

"As often as they see me," he joked. "One year, our mom offered to keep Hannah during the summer, but Hannah had a tough time being away from home."

"Then she and her father are close?"

"As close as they can be when Mitch is out of town so much," he said wryly.

"Hannah told me her mother died three years ago."

"She had an inoperable brain tumor and went quickly. After that, Mitch fell apart. I stepped in to help him with Hannah. Marcy's sister had offered to take her, but we talked it over and he decided he didn't want her living so far away in Utah with an aunt she hardly knew."

"He's lucky you're willing and able to fill the gap."

Trey grinned. "I tell him that all the time, but I'm not certain he believes me. Maybe he should hear it from you."

Their drinks arrived and after ordering the house specialty—Philly steak sandwiches and home fries—he asked, "If Hannah and I hadn't needed your help last week, would you have ever agreed to go out with me?"

"No," she answered promptly.

"Are you saying I couldn't have worn you down?"

He seemed surprised and she debated the wisdom of sugarcoating the truth, but being less than honest only lumped her in the same category of other women who merely told him what they thought he wanted to hear.

"Oh, you're a very charming, interesting man," she admitted lightly, "but charm wasn't in your favor."

"Really?"

"Really. From past experience, I've learned that charming men are very self-centered, superficial and untrustworthy."

He winced as he clutched his chest. "Ouch."

She smiled at his theatrics. "The truth hurts."

"It does. What changed your mind? At least, I assume you changed your mind since you're with me now."

She smiled. "You have Hannah to thank. Any man who gives his niece as much time and attention as you do can't be *all* bad."

He raised his bottle and clinked it against her wineglass. "Now, that is something to celebrate."

Their meals came and as they ate, Sierra discovered Trey had season tickets to the baseball and football games. He was a fan of country music, and had just participated in the annual Escape to the Lake bike run, which covered one hundred and fifty miles over two days and raised money for the National Multiple Sclerosis Society.

"Maybe you can join me next year," he said enthusiastically.

"That seems a daunting trip for someone who hasn't been on a bicycle in years. Maybe I'll do my part by contributing to your pledge fund."

"Chicken." He grinned.

She smiled back. "Glutton for punishment. Now, if you and Hannah ever take a sedate ride around the park, call me."

"I'll do it," he promised.

Sensing the time to talk about Hannah had arrived, Sierra drew a bracing breath and began. "Remember when you asked me why I'd played along with your charade last week?"

His eyes narrowed slightly. "Yeah."

"Well, I sort of had an ulterior motive. It didn't concern you," she hastened to add. "It was because of Hannah."

"Hannah? Why?"

Again, she knew she had to be careful how she broached the subject. Trey would probably think of her worries as a personal attack on his parenting skills, and she didn't want that, at all.

"Has she seen a doctor lately? Had a school physical, perhaps?"

"Not that I know of. Why?"

"She seems a little scrawny for her age."

Trey heard the hesitation in Sierra's voice, and he hurried to reassure her. "Her mother was petite, too. She was a dancer so she also was a nutrition nut. I'm sure Hannah takes after her."

"Maybe," she answered, her tone as noncommittal as her word choice. "I understand skinny, but I also noticed how she only picks at her food. Given how much she exercises and practices her dance steps, I'd expect her to have a heartier appetite."

"She's always been a finicky eater."

"There's finicky and then there's *finicky*. I believe she's beyond both."

He didn't appreciate or like Sierra's implication. "What are you saying?" he demanded. "Spell it out."

"I'm only suggesting—"

"Do you suspect she's anorexic?" he demanded.

"She might be," she defended, "which is why I'd asked about a physical and why I observed her so closely last week. I could be wrong, but it doesn't hurt to watch her at dinnertime or arrange for a pediatrician visit, does it?"

He hated the idea of Hannah having a problem he'd overlooked. He was a physician, for God's sake. It was his job to notice things and he took pride in being observant. On the other hand, he hadn't noticed Mitch hadn't been coping with Marcy's death as well as his brother had claimed until Trey had dropped by unannounced and found seven-year-old Hannah dragging a trash can full of beer and whiskey bottles to the street for pickup.

No, he was more attentive to his family these days. Sierra was wrong. Completely and unquestionably wrong.

"I spend most evenings with her. I see her eat all the time," he snapped.

"I spent time with her, too," she reminded him. "From

what I saw, she doesn't eat. She dawdles. She scoots her food back and forth so it *appears* as if she's eaten. She cuts her food into tinier and tinier pieces so people think the food has disappeared. Can you honestly say you've actually seen her swallow more than a few bites? I can't."

Now that she'd pointed it out, he'd never seen Hannah clean her plate or eat a complete serving of anything. His friends complained about how their kids ate them out of house and home, but he couldn't say the same about Hannah. He'd talked to Mitch about it once, but Mitch had assured him she was her mother's daughter in that regard.

"She claims she's a picky eater," Sierra continued, "but she has to love *something,* even if it's only a fast-food hamburger meal. When we were at the grocery store last week she didn't ask for any of the junk food kids usually want. In fact, she was quite ambivalent about our selections. If you hadn't been with us, our cart would have only held a gallon of milk."

"She dances, like her mother," he defended, certain Sierra was overreacting. "Hannah's just trying to follow in her footsteps, which means eating good healthy foods instead of stuff filled with empty calories."

"The key word is *eating,* Trey. Now, maybe she snacks and then isn't hungry for dinner, but I offered her things like celery and carrot sticks instead of chips, fresh fruit instead of candy or cookies, but she declined those, too."

He didn't recall Hannah ever snacking either. But how could Sierra presume to suggest she saw a problem when he didn't? Irritated by the notion, he ground out, "You've been with Hannah how many times over how many days? How does a handful of encounters make you an expert?"

She placed a hand on his arm. "It doesn't. I admit I may be way off base—"

"You are."

"I only see what I see, but you know her habits better than I do. Maybe she chows down like a field hand when she's with her dad. She's a sensitive young lady and maybe when he's gone, she's too nervous to be hungry. Personally, I think she's grown quite adept at hiding how little she eats."

"Don't you think you're overreacting? She's only ten. What ten-year-old can keep a secret of that nature?"

"They're young, not stupid," she informed him. "I'm simply saying you need to be mindful and vigilant. Then, if you decide she has a problem, you can deal with it." She paused. "And if she doesn't have one, you can rub my nose in my mistake and say, 'I told you so.'"

He raked his hair with one hand. "Okay. I'll look into it."

"I care about Hannah and I wouldn't have mentioned this if I wasn't worried about her."

The irony of his attitude struck him full force. Earlier today, he'd been pleased because she'd been so conscientious about Hannah's feelings. How could he tear her to shreds now, when concern for Hannah was still her motive?

He'd tried so hard to steer his brother down the straight and narrow path for the past three years, but if Sierra was correct and he'd missed the obvious, he'd feel as if he'd let his family down.

Sierra had to be wrong. There had to be a logical explanation, although none came to mind. Meanwhile, it wouldn't hurt to follow Sierra's advice to watch and observe. He'd also talk to his brother, ask a few pointed questions, and that would be the end of it.

At least, he *hoped* that would be the end. Knowing how Mitch didn't seem to handle stress or problems very well these days, who knew what would happen if he knew his daughter had an eating disorder. The idea could easily be more than he could, or would want, to handle. If that were the case, Mitch might decide to finally follow through on his threat to send Hannah to Marcy's sister in Utah—a threat Trey had been fighting off and on since Marcy had died.

On the other hand, perhaps thinking his daughter might have a problem would convince him to focus on Hannah instead of himself for a change. Perhaps he'd finally realize how much his little girl needed *him,* not her uncle or an aunt she'd only seen a handful of times.

Either way, he would have to tread lightly. He'd already lost enough people in his life. Losing Hannah was not an option.

"I'll look into it," he said.

"See that you do, Trey." Her tone was harsh. "I know you don't want to believe me, but I'm not a novice at this. My little sister suffered from anorexia, too. She was much older than Hannah when food became an issue, but her symptoms were remarkably similar."

Her revelation shocked him. "Your sister?" he asked faintly.

"She was sixteen when we noticed she had a problem. I'd come home from college for Christmas break of my freshman year and I was shocked by how much she'd changed since I'd left in the fall. My parents got her into therapy, but she didn't learn how to manage her disorder overnight. To this day, she still has to be careful when she's in stressful situations. So, don't postpone acting on this if you find I'm right. Eating disorders don't disappear on their own."

He might have been able to dismiss Sierra's worries but, given her background and personal experience, he couldn't. "I'll handle it," he said grimly.

"And you'll ask your brother to be alert, too?"

He already visualized the upcoming battle, but it would have to be fought. For Hannah's sake. "I'll talk to him."

CHAPTER SIX

WHILE Trey had been polite and upheld his end of the conversation, Sierra could tell he was preoccupied. She didn't blame him. Hannah meant a great deal to him and although he'd denied the possibility she had an eating disorder, the idea clearly weighed on his mind.

As she followed him out of the restaurant, she was surprised by how much she hated to see these hours come to an end. More importantly, she was disappointed that her relationship with Hannah probably would, too. Trey was hearty and whole, and certainly didn't need her help any longer.

It had felt good to be needed—not for her medical knowledge, but for herself. She'd love to continue being a part of their lives, but she doubted if Trey would allow it. He was too determined to be the one in charge, the one in complete control, which was why she wasn't surprised by how he'd responded to her next suggestion...

"If you'd like me to talk to Hannah or her father, I'd be happy to—"

"I appreciate the offer, but—"

"You'll deal with it." She grinned outwardly, but inwardly she sighed with disappointment. "I know. If you should change your mind, call me."

His nod could have meant anything, so she changed the subject. "Thanks for a lovely evening. I had a nice time."

"We'll do it again. Soon."

"I'd like that," she said simply. "Goodnight, Trey."

As she started down the sidewalk, he called out after her. "Where are you going?"

"To the bus stop."

"I'll drive you home."

"That isn't necessary."

"I'm driving you home," he said firmly.

"Really, Trey—"

"Come on. My car is just as close as the bus stop and it has the added bonus of no waiting."

She would wait, she knew, because according to her watch the bus was pulling away from the curb now. The next wouldn't arrive for another thirty minutes and the idea of a delay suddenly seemed distasteful. "All right."

"Is a bus pass that much cheaper than a parking permit?" he asked as they strolled toward the car lot.

"Not a lot, but riding mass transportation eliminates the extra expenses of gasoline, oil changes, wear and tear on the car, tires, etcetera."

"Ah, you're a frugal woman."

She could have laughed off his comment and given an inane one of her own, but the urge to share was strong. Normally, she would have squelched that feeling immediately. Trust didn't come easily for her anymore, thanks to David, but she sensed Trey suffered from the same disorder she did. He hadn't jumped for joy when Hannah had dragged her into the Donovan family life and yet he'd allowed it, knowing she'd discover personal things about his family that few people, if any, did. It was her turn to take a chance…

"I have to be," she admitted. "I told you I had a few debts, right? Well, for the last three years of our marriage I'd suspected David was living a lifestyle far beyond our means. He was a financial planner and always regaled me with how well his investments did in the markets or how profitable a new money-making opportunity had become, but little things didn't add up. I eventually spoke to him, repeatedly, but he always had a ready excuse. I talked to his family and they accused me of being jealous of his success, which wasn't the case, of course.

"Then, after he died, my fears came true. Credit cards were charged to the max. His investments and capital ventures were worthless. To make matters worse, because he'd committed suicide, his life insurance wouldn't pay his death benefit."

Those days had been horrible. She'd been struggling to do her job and when she'd gone home, she'd been flooded with bills in the mail and bombarded by creditors on the phone. She'd experienced every possible emotion during that time—from shock to fury—until their accountant helped her sort out her finances, leaving her with nothing to show for her marriage but a hefty repayment schedule and a healthy distrust of captivating men.

"Saddling you with the debt."

"*Mountains* of it," she corrected. "I sold everything we owned—the house, the cars, the vacation home, even my jewelry—but it wasn't enough."

"Didn't his family help you?"

"Heavens, no. They'd conveniently forgotten I'd asked them to intervene and instead blamed me because he took his own life. According to them, I should have seen the signs he was in trouble and gotten help. Maybe I should have, but he was gone every evening, wining and dining his clients. I rarely saw him, which is why we had problems we couldn't resolve."

"It takes both parties to fix a relationship."

"I know," she admitted, "but I still feel as if I should have done more."

Although she knew David would never have agreed to counseling—it hadn't been in his nature to admit he had a problem of any sort—she would always live with the guilt and the what-ifs. Which was why she'd risked sharing her worries about Hannah. She hadn't been able to help David deal with his problems, but she could certainly do her best to help Hannah with hers.

"That must have hurt, to listen to his family's accusations."

"It did at first, but you have to love someone for him or her to hurt you. They'd never been supportive of our marriage, so we simply tolerated each other. I wasn't in the same social class, you see, and they had such high hopes for their son. Being paired with a lowly doctor didn't fit their criteria.

"In any event…" She cleared her throat and continued, "I learned my lesson for next time and I pinch my pennies until they squeak."

"Then it's a good thing my chauffeur service is inexpensive."

"How inexpensive is *inexpensive?*" she asked.

"Oh, a cup of coffee should cover the cost."

She smiled. "Fair enough."

She recited her address and he drove there without asking for directions.

Sierra leaned against the seat cushions, feeling more relaxed and at peace than she had in a long time. Unburdening herself had been more cathartic than she'd expected. Although Trey probably didn't know what his sympathetic ear had done for her, she was profoundly grateful.

To her surprise, awareness soon hitched a ride with her contentment and gratitude.

What once had seemed like a roomy car now seemed cramped, which was odd because they'd sat in this same vehicle together a few short days ago, with Hannah in the backseat, too. Now, however, the atmosphere was completely different because she was seeing him through appreciative eyes.

He looked fantastic in his jeans and polo shirt. He smelled better, his personal scent more powerful in the enclosed space. Best of all, his velvety deep voice reminded her of melted chocolate.

She recited her rule to steer clear of charming men.

Rules are made to be broken.

Watching his hands lightly grip the steering-wheel sent

her imagination into overdrive. What would it feel like to experience his touch, not in a clinical way but personally, intimately?

Her own hands shook in her eagerness to stroke his muscular thigh, not as his physician this time but as his lover.

Don't be ridiculous, her rational side reminded her. Just because she didn't feel weighed down by her previous life, she shouldn't act precipitously. So what if he was kind to his niece and had been thoughtful enough to take her to dinner? While both were acceptable deeds on his part, she would be foolish to do something she'd only regret later.

To her dismay, her argument had little effect on her raging hormones. She threaded her fingers together to keep them from wandering where her instincts begged to go. To dispel a sudden, intense ache inside her, she shifted positions and crossed her legs for good measure.

Rain began to fall, first in drops then at a steady rate, which only enhanced the cozy feeling. As he braked in front of her apartment, her reckless side wanted to circle the block a few more times while her logical part begged her to jump from the car and not look back.

She was tired of being logical. She wanted to be impetuous, if only to prove to herself that she still could be.

"Hang on while I get my umbrella," he told her.

"That's okay," she said. "I won't melt."

As they dashed up her walk and onto the porch, she remained conscious of his firm grip on her elbow. Feeling like a teenager on her first date, Sierra clumsily dug in her purse for her house keys. Her heart was racing ridiculously fast and she heard herself breathing. Or was she hearing Trey's ragged breaths?

"Here they are," she said, holding them aloft as she stole a glance at him. To her surprise, his expression was almost grim, as if he'd struggled to climb the stairs. If she didn't know better, she'd think he was completely out of shape, but a man who participated in a 150-mile bike trek wouldn't have problems racing along twenty feet and up eight steps.

He suddenly exhaled one deep, audible breath. When he spoke, his voice was raspy and harsh. "I changed my mind about the coffee."

"It's your knee, isn't it?" His injury was the only explanation she could think of to explain his pained expression.

He shook his head, his gaze intent. "Coming inside isn't a good idea. I'll want more than coffee."

Passion flared in his eyes—the same passion she felt for him. The idea was thrilling. Daunting. Dangerous.

"I don't think either of us are ready for that right now," he added.

Great. She'd met a man who cranked her hormones to full steam, a man who made her remember how wonderful it felt to seize the moment, and he had a conscience. While part of her whined over her unfulfilled needs, another part was impressed—not to mention grateful—that one of them was thinking with his head instead of his body parts.

"You understand, don't you?"

She was torn between disappointment and relief. "Yeah, I do."

His smile was small, as if he fought the same war within himself, before he lowered his head to kiss her. It was a remarkably chaste kiss, but it contained everything from an electrical snap and sizzle to a promise of future fulfillment, and she felt every sensation clear down to her toes.

"Goodnight, Sierra," he murmured before he turned abruptly and dashed down the stairs.

She went inside and waited until the throaty purr of his car faded into the distance. Slowly, she walked into the living room and dumped her purse on the side chair, wishing he'd stayed and relieved that he hadn't.

Obviously Trey didn't see her as a challenge to overcome as David had. Instead of taking what she'd freely offered, he'd gone the more cautious and gentlemanly route.

Stop comparing the two men, she scolded as she sank onto her recliner. *Apples and oranges may both be fruit, but they aren't the same.*

In the past week, she'd seen depths to Trey's character that she'd never seen in David's. Tonight, she'd seen *restraint*—a word which also had not been a part of her husband's vocabulary. If it had, she wouldn't have landed in the position of paying off debt or facing bankruptcy.

In any case, as much as she missed the intimacy of the early days of her marriage, she couldn't rush into a relationship of any sort without calculating the cost. It was a lesson her marriage had taught her, and one which she would never forget.

Trey wondered if he'd finally lost his mind. He'd been in the company of a beautiful woman, enough electricity had been generated between the two of them to raise every hair on his head and he'd walked away.

No, he thought wryly, he'd *run*.

He must be nuts.

Walking away wasn't anything new for him. Flirtatious women were as common as old shoes, and back in high school he'd learned how to politely fend off the girls. The few who'd interested him he'd taken out, but he was always very careful about how his evenings ended. Through the years, he'd enjoyed a physical relationship with several—he didn't claim to be celibate—but he'd never been willing to tie himself down. His career required responsibility and he wanted one area of his life to remain free of any entanglements.

Marcy's death had changed that, too. He'd taken on the part-time responsibility of his niece, which meant his personal life wasn't as carefree as it once had been. And after seeing how his solid, dependable big brother had changed so completely after losing the love of his life, he'd decided the status quo was just fine for him.

At times, though, he envied his brother for enjoying a wonderful, fulfilling relationship while it had lasted, packed full of memories that could never be stolen.

Making memories with Sierra sounded…good. No, it sounded more than good. It sounded *perfect*.

And he'd walked away.

It had been the right thing to do, he thought as he drove down the street. Kissing her, feeling her softness and tasting her warm lips had only enhanced his craving for more of the same. Walking into her apartment, availing himself of more than a cup of coffee, would have complicated matters further. He had enough problems in his life right now.

Problems or not, he had to admit how well Sierra had fit into his life. Not only did he look forward to her company and conversation, but Hannah had plainly considered Sierra to be her friend as much as his. Previously, his niece had only tolerated his dates and had uttered the most long-suffering sigh if he'd invited someone over, which was why he'd stopped doing so, but she would count the hours until Sierra had arrived.

On Saturday, they'd parked him on a bench with a magazine and a bottle of water while they'd trawled a shopping center for inexpensive baubles, bottles of nail polish and the latest teen-idol movie poster. When they'd finished spending Hannah's earnings, the two had giggled for hours as they'd accessorized her clothes, painted toe- and fingernails, and tacked three new posters to her bedroom walls.

As much time as the two had spent together, maybe Sierra *had* seen a troubling behavior in his niece that he'd missed. There was only one way to find out.

He flicked on his turn signal and swung into a different traffic lane. Talking to Mitch had to be done and he may as well do it now. Chances were, he'd see his niece slurping down a huge milk shake and that would end this whole nonsense.

"Uncle Trey," Hannah screeched as she opened the door to him. "What are you doing here?"

"I missed you, short stuff." He tugged on her ponytail.

Her smile lit up her face. "You saw me yesterday."

"I know. I wanted to see you again. What's your dad doing?"

"Watching TV," she said. "I'm making brownies. He loves my brownies, you know."

He'd walked into the perfect experiment to disprove Sierra's theory. "I do, too."

"Then you're just in time because they're almost ready." In the distance, the timer beeped. "That's them." She dashed off, leaving Trey to find his brother.

"What's up?" Mitch asked as he clicked off the television.

"I wanted to drop by. Touch base with you about a few things."

"Like what?"

Trey hesitated as he wondered how to broach the subject. Fortunately, he didn't have to because Hannah walked in at that moment with a tray holding brownies and glasses of her famous lemonade. "Be careful," she told them. "The dessert's still hot."

Trey noticed there were only two of each. "Where's yours?" he asked her.

"Oh, I'm eating mine in the kitchen after it cools down." *She's grown quite adept at hiding how little she eats.*

"I drove all this way to visit and you're going to hang out in the kitchen?" He shook his head melodramatically. "I'm crushed."

"Aw, Uncle Trey..."

"Join us," he invited. "Your brownie can cool in here as easily as it'll cool in the kitchen."

She frowned. "I made them for my dad, not for me."

Another warning bell clanged.

"Surely he won't mind if you eat one piece?" Trey coaxed. "Will you, Mitch?"

Mitch waved his hand, apparently unconcerned by the exchange. "Sure, hon. I hope you don't expect me to eat the whole pan by myself." He patted his stomach. "I have to watch my waistline, too, you know."

Trey spoke with his brother over his upcoming travel schedule while he waited for Hannah. Finally, she trudged in with her own saucer, looking as if he was asking her to eat an earthworm rather than a gooey chocolate brownie.

Instead of the generous square on his own plate, her portion was bite-size.

"This is delicious, Hannah," Mitch gushed as he downed his serving. "You're a great cook, honey. I don't know what I'd do without you."

Hannah preened under his praise. "Oh, Daddy."

"This is good," Trey confirmed. "Aren't you going to taste it for yourself?"

"Oh, I licked the bowl clean," she said airily. "I know how brownies taste."

"Yes, but the batter isn't quite the same as the finished product."

Dutifully, she nibbled. Trey noticed the piece she returned to her plate couldn't have been missing more than a few crumbs. A mouse or a bird would have taken a larger bite.

"Daddy, can I go upstairs now? I have to practice my dance routine."

"Sure, hon, go ahead."

"'Bye, Uncle Trey." Immediately, she bounded up the stairs to her room.

Trey saw the minuscule brownie she'd left behind and his spirits plummeted. Sierra's concerns might not be as far off the mark as he'd thought or hoped.

"What did you want to touch base with me about?" Mitch asked.

Trey studied his brother. His dark hair was threaded with silver and his face was more lined than a few months ago. He looked tired, but it wasn't a physical tiredness. It was more a mental exhaustion that caused him to look at least ten years older than he was.

He missed his happy-go-lucky brother—the one who'd smiled easily, laughed often and embraced life with gusto. He missed the brother who'd constantly told him to settle down with one woman because marriage was a wonderful thing. He missed the brother who'd taken it upon himself to dole out advice freely based on the wisdom his extra year of living had given him.

Instead, their roles had been reversed. Trey had become the older brother/caretaker and had begun to believe he'd play that part for a long time.

The whole situation was so sad and so damn frustrating. Sure, he understood Mitch was hurting, but three years of mourning was ridiculous. He'd suggested counseling numerous times and would do so again, but not today. Today was for Mitch and Marcy's daughter.

"I wanted to talk about Hannah," Trey began.

"What about her?"

"Have you noticed she doesn't eat like most kids her age?"

Mitch shrugged. "She's a picky eater. Marcy was the same way. You know that."

Trey wondered now if Marcy had suffered from an eating disorder, too. Could Hannah have either intentionally or subconsciously absorbed enough of her mother's habits to affect her now? Habits that on the surface seemed healthy but in actuality weren't?

"True, but take tonight, for instance. Most kids would have eaten a brownie—a *big* brownie—without any hesitation. She didn't put enough in her mouth to taste it."

Mitch shrugged. "What can I say? She's very weight conscious because she's a dancer. If everyone had half as much self-control as she did, there wouldn't be an obesity problem in this country."

What Trey had seen today went beyond self-control. "Let me ask you this. What did she eat for dinner tonight? Or lunch this afternoon?"

"I don't know. I'd run an errand and she ate lunch while I was gone."

Trey recognized another ploy and felt guilty for taking Hannah's reassurances at face value for far too long. "What about dinner?"

"We had grilled chicken and pasta, and a lettuce salad."

"Did she clean her plate?"

"She never does. You know that." Mitch leaned forward. "What's all this about?"

"Sierra thinks—"

"Is this the same Sierra who Hannah talks about constantly? The new doctor you're working with?"

"Yes. Sierra thinks—and I'm inclined to agree with her—Hannah might have an eating disorder."

Mitch sat back in his chair wearing a disgusted expression. "You people. Always looking for problems because you have M.D. after your name. Well, you're wrong. Being petite and fine-boned, avoiding snacks and exercising doesn't make her anorexic."

"No, but—"

"She eats when she's with me. Maybe she doesn't when she's with you, and if that's the case, maybe we need to rethink our child-care arrangement."

Clearly Mitch was in a defensive mood, but Trey wasn't in the best of spirits either. As much as he wanted to argue, that attitude wouldn't be beneficial. He couldn't alienate his brother and risk losing access to Hannah, so he forced himself to remain calm and use the charm he'd carefully honed over the years.

"There's nothing wrong with our arrangement," he told Mitch. "I love having Hannah around. If she eats at home and not when she's with me, we'll have to talk to her. Meanwhile, I'm asking you to observe her habits so we can compare notes. You're a pharmacist," Trey continued. "You know the long-lasting effects of an eating disorder. If—" he stressed the word "—if Hannah has a problem, you'd want to deal with it before her health is compromised, wouldn't you?"

Mitch frowned then finally nodded. "What am I looking for?"

"She'll appear as if she's eating, but she isn't," he said, reciting the points Sierra had stated earlier. "Most of her food will end up in the garbage disposal, but she'll be quick enough to dispose of the evidence without you seeing how much she's thrown away."

Once again, he was reminded of the meals when Hannah had jumped up to clear the table as soon as he'd laid his own fork across his plate. He'd always thought she'd been impatient to dive into her spare-time activities. Now the motivation behind her impatience was suspect.

"I'll watch her, but I still think you're wrong about her being anorexic."

"Let's hope I am." Trey prayed it would be so. "We'll talk again on Friday to figure out what comes next."

Mitch rubbed his face tiredly. "I guess."

"I'm serious, Mitch. We have to develop a game plan, even if it's nothing more than scheduling an appointment with her pediatrician and the therapist she used to see."

"Okay, okay. I think you're overreacting, but we'll talk on Friday."

Trey sensed the time had come to change the subject. He'd mentioned his concerns and set a deadline for action, which was all he could do for now. He could take it upon himself to confront Hannah, but asking her pointed questions could backfire. If she knew they were watching her, she'd only become more creative at hiding her habits. As Sierra had said, Hannah was young, not stupid.

An incident with one brownie wasn't enough for a diagnosis. He simply had to set aside his preconceived notions of what was "normal" for Hannah and watch for a pattern as Sierra had. Then pray Mitch would allow him to intervene.

"Dr. McAllaster…" one of the nurses stopped her in the hallway the next morning "…Dr. Donovan would like you to admit this patient."

Although Sierra had seen Trey off and on ever since she'd reported for duty, knowing he'd asked for her caused her heart to skip a beat. She quickly willed herself to ignore it because she didn't have time to pander to such foolish personal reactions. She'd been running from room to room ever since she'd arrived and the stack of clipboards on the in-pile hadn't decreased.

"He doesn't need my signature to admit someone," she pointed out.

Billie, a nurse in her forties, looked uncomfortable. "In this case, he, um, sort of does."

Sierra narrowed her gaze. "Why?"

"Dr. Madison says there are only two free beds in the medical unit and he won't accept this patient. From what I overheard, he and Dr. Donovan exchanged words."

She could imagine the scene. William was using his power to thwart Trey's crusader attitude for no other reason than he could. Men could be such children…and knowing how nasty William could be at times, she guessed he'd grown up without sharing his toys.

"I presume Dr. Donovan thinks I can twist Dr. Madison's arm."

Billie nodded, her gaze both hopeful and beseeching. "I think so. Anyway, Dr. Donovan wasn't getting anywhere, so he asked for an internal medicine consult."

She recognized his tactic. He didn't need her opinion because he already knew what the patient needed, but by asking for it he'd gain more ammunition for his side.

Just like David.

Not quite, she corrected herself, trying to be fair. Maybe he *was* using her as his back door because he couldn't enter through the front, but his motives weren't selfish. Unlike David, Trey was working the system for his patient's benefit—not his own—and she'd do the same if the situation were reversed.

"I'll see what I can do." Sierra accepted the clipboard and began scanning Billie's and Trey's recorded notes.

"Thanks." Billie turned. "Oh, before you go in, you might want to use this." She handed her a blue vial of mentholated cream.

Sierra eyed the jar. A pinch of the salve rubbed under one's nose effectively blocked out offensive odors. "That bad, eh?"

"Oh, yeah."

Sierra dropped the jar into her pocket. "Thanks, but I'll try to suffer through without it."

"Suit yourself, but don't say I didn't warn you."

As soon as Sierra opened the door, a noxious odor of unwashed body greeted her. A man in mismatched, filthy clothing lay on the bed. His beard was ragged, his cheekbones sunken and his smile toothless. According to the form in her hand, he was forty-two, but he could have easily passed for seventy.

"Hello, Sam," she said to the man, careful to breathe through her mouth. "I'm Dr. McAllaster. Dr. Donovan asked me to review your case."

"Suit yourself."

Sierra glanced at Trey's scrawl and tried to decipher the words. "How long have you had these sores on your legs?" She folded back his ragged pant legs and saw the ulcerated flesh that extended from his ankles to his knees.

"A month or so. Dr. Donovan gave me some stuff to smear on when I came in last time, but I lost the tube."

Or sold it, she thought, before she realized the details didn't matter. Gone was gone.

"'Twasn't helpin' anyways," he added.

"Do you remember how these sores started?"

"Ran across thorny bushes of some sort," he said. "Got scratched up pretty bad. I had to get me some new pants from the mission, too. What was bad was I had 'em broke in," he mourned.

This pair wasn't exactly interview attire, so she shuddered to imagine what his old pair had been like. Returning to the notes, she saw his leukocyte count was elevated, indicating his body was trying to fight off an infection that his poor hygiene had only aggravated. Trey had requested a blood culture to rule out septicemia, but that test required a minimum of six hours before a preliminary result would be available and often required twenty-four. This poor man was definitely a candidate for high-powered antibiotics, regardless of what the culture showed. If he didn't already have bacteria circulating in his blood, without proper treatment, he soon would.

Unfortunately, the best way to deliver treatment was debatable.

She understood all too clearly why Will Madison had butted heads with Trey over this patient. Anyone else presenting with these symptoms would have been a candidate for home health nursing care and she would have been the first to make that recommendation. Sam, however, was a special case with extenuating circumstances and one she'd seen far too often in metropolitan emergency rooms. As much as she hated to dispute Lane Keegan's directive, Sam would be better served with inpatient care.

She smiled at the man. "You need aggressive therapy, Sam, if we're going to heal these lesions."

He nodded. "Figured as much. Like I told the doc, if you'll give me some pills, I'll be on my way."

"I'll talk to Dr. Donovan and we'll see what we can arrange for you," she hedged. Pills would help, but an oral antibiotic would provide only part of the treatment. "Someone will be right back."

"Not goin' nowhere," he said as he lay against the pillows and closed his eyes.

Trey, on the other hand, had disappeared.

"Where did he go?" she asked Billie.

"Radiology, I think. Why?"

"Sam Pulaski," she said bluntly. "As soon as Dr. Donovan returns, I have to see him."

"Will do. What am I supposed to do about Sam in the meantime?"

Sierra weighed her options. "Give him a thorough scrubbing. If I can get him admitted, and that's a very big if, the people upstairs will thank us. As soon as he's less…" she wrinkled her nose "…noxious, start an IV so we can push antibiotics."

"What if he isn't admitted?"

Sierra didn't want to consider that possibility. "Let's think positive, shall we?"

Billie didn't appear eager to follow her orders. "Maybe we should wait until—"

"The man needs treatment and we'll see he gets it. Meanwhile, there's no need for everyone to smell *that* for the rest of the day, is there?"

"I guess not."

On her way to the nurses' station, Sierra ran into Trey. His lazy grin and the twinkle in his eyes made her feel as if she were the one woman he'd been waiting to see since he'd risen that morning—the one woman who'd made all the problems in his day fade into insignificance.

Don't be silly. The man smiles like that at everyone, she scolded herself, but her admonition didn't hold back her rising spirits or slow down her galloping pulse rate. She simply smiled back, pleased they were finally able to exchange a few private words.

"How was the rest of your evening?" he asked.

"Quiet." *Lonely.* "What about you?"

"I stopped by Mitch's on my way home."

Her curiosity demanded information. "And?"

Two nurses walked by, followed by an orderly pushing an elderly lady in a wheelchair. "I'll tell you later," he said as he guided her to one side of the hallway so the traffic didn't run over them. "Have you had a chance to see Sam Pulaski?"

"I just did. By the way, I don't appreciate being caught in the middle."

"What do you mean?" He sounded innocent.

"You know exactly what I mean, Trey Donovan. You should have called upstairs and told them Sam was coming. End of story."

"Now, why didn't I think of that?" he asked wryly.

"It's what you always did to me," she reminded him.

"No, I always invited you to Emergency to examine the patient *before* I sent him or her upstairs. For the record, I gave Will the same courtesy."

Obviously, Will had been his usual uncooperative self. "He wouldn't come," she guessed.

"Wouldn't come and wouldn't even *consider* coming," he said, his eyes turning dark with suppressed fury. "Which was why I pulled you in as a consulting. He won't be able to turn down a request from you."

"You honestly believe I have more clout?"

"You're both in the same service," he pointed out. "It's more difficult for him to refuse your request than it apparently is to refuse mine."

Great. She was caught in the middle of a power struggle, forced to choose between doing what she *wanted* to do and what she *should* do. However it ended, someone wouldn't be happy.

CHAPTER SEVEN

"You're giving me far too much credit," Sierra stated. "Will can say no to me as easily as you."

"Yeah, but he'll at least listen to your arguments. I, on the other hand, don't receive the same consideration."

"Why not?"

"He's still aggravated at me for your transfer. As long as you're down here, he has to cover two units instead of one. According to him, you were assigned to screen out the unnecessary admissions." He raised an eyebrow. "Is that true, because that isn't how I read the memo?"

Obviously, the two men differed on their interpretation. "Yes and no. I'm supposed to, and I quote, 'foster the use of the newly expanded Outpatient Resources for non-emergent cases, ensuring the Inpatient Resources are reserved for those with life-threatening conditions.' Which means—"

"I know what it means. Anybody who can possibly be treated at home without risk is to be followed through the outpatient clinic. I get that. *All* of my emergency physicians get that because it's what we've always done, but septicemia *is* life-threatening."

"We don't know he's progressed that far."

"You're willing to wait until bacteria are swimming around his bloodstream, finding a safe haven in his heart, lungs or other organs?" He sounded incredulous.

"Of course not," she denied. "If I was in Will's position, I would have taken Sam without question. You know that. In all fairness to him, though, Sam technically doesn't warrant a hospital admission. Nursing care, yes, but not an admission."

"Just where is he supposed to get nursing care and sterile dressings?"

"Home health, the outpatient clinic."

"Home health, eh? The man's homeless. Do we list his address as the fourth park bench past the Panther Hollow Run footbridge in Schenley Park? Or tell the nurses to hunt for him in the third cardboard box behind the nearest shopping center?"

"Of course not, but Sam could visit the clinic for daily dressing changes and—"

"And how does he keep those bandages clean from one day to the next?" he demanded. "He'll be constantly exposed to bacteria and we'll never gain the upper hand with his infection."

"You don't have to convince me," she said. "I'm only trying to explain Will's point of view. His bed space is limited and if Sam can be treated elsewhere—"

"In my medical judgment, he can't. The question is, where do *you* stand?"

Sierra felt the squeeze of being in the middle. For an instant she wondered about Trey's motives. Was he looking out for Sam, or was he more interested in winning because of ego?

"I know it looks as if my pride is getting in the way," he said, as if he'd read her mind, "but Sam takes care of himself in a hit-and-miss fashion. He might drop in at the outpatient clinic, but I doubt if he will. For some reason, he trusts me. I can't let him down."

Theoretically and academically, she agreed with Will. However, from a moral, humane standpoint, she couldn't disagree with Trey. If they didn't attack Sam's problem aggressively, he would return to Emergency in a few days or weeks and in far worse shape.

She sighed. "I'll see what I can do."

His smile transformed his face. "Thanks."

As he headed down the hall with a jaunty step, Sierra commandeered a vacant chair at the nurses' station and called her colleague. "I have a patient down here who needs—"

"No can do," he replied. "I don't have a free bed."

"Come on, Will. I checked the computer and there are two available."

"Not for long. I'm expecting a guy from the OP clinic with a FUO."

Fever of undetermined origin meant a thorough workup. "You still have one more," she reminded him.

"Yeah, and I'm saving it for an emergency."

Sierra gritted her teeth. "I'm working in Emergency, remember? My case is just as important—"

"Is this the guy with the leg ulcers?"

"Yes."

"I already told Donovan there was no room at the inn."

"Look at this case from Trey's viewpoint."

"Sorry. Give the guy some antibiotics and send him to the outpatient clinic for an IV. Better yet, plug him into the home-health network and they can do the dressing changes, etcetera, there."

Sierra wondered if Will would be as eager to refer Sam to another physician if he were the Mayor of Pittsburgh instead of one of its homeless citizens.

"His lifestyle is part of the problem. Please, Will," she wheedled, "can't you find space for this guy? Maybe send someone home a little early?"

He didn't answer. Sierra hoped his silence meant he was considering her suggestion.

"Does he have a positive blood culture?"

"It's too soon to know for certain."

"If it isn't positive, then—"

"If it isn't positive today, then it will be tomorrow or the day after," she retorted. "Would you rather we nip this in the bud, or wait until he's in worse shape before you get him?"

"Does he have any underlying condition? Uncontrolled diabetes? Hypertension?"

She checked the chart. "No."

"Look, Sierra, my hands are tied. I'd help if I could, but it sounds as if he'd manage just as well under the care of the clinic."

"You realize you leave me no choice but to go to Dr. Keegan."

"Be my guest," he encouraged. "He'll agree with me. Without lab results to support a systemic infection, Keegan won't budge. I know because I just went through this with a family-practice patient yesterday. My only other suggestion is to wait a few hours. If his blood culture turns positive, we'll talk."

"And if it doesn't?"

"Mind you, I'm not promising anything, but I have a diabetic who, if his blood sugars don't tank, might be able to go home. If he does, I'll have room."

"Thanks, Will. I appreciate it."

"There's a catch, though," he warned.

Here it comes. She braced herself for something unsavory. "What?"

"This guy has to arrive in mint condition. My staff doesn't have time to administer the full beauty treatment. We don't do makeovers up here."

Sierra wanted to argue that her department wasn't a salon either, but as they were already working on Sam's personal hygiene, she didn't object to his terms. "Done."

"And if I take any flak for this decision, tell Donovan I'm sending a lot of it his way."

"I'll tell him."

"And you'll owe me."

Sierra winced. Of all the things he'd asked for, she hated owing Will Madison anything. "Sure."

"Good. I'll keep in touch."

Sierra disconnected the call just as Trey joined her. "Your expression suggests good news," he said.

"It depends on your perspective," she answered. "Will wants us to wait a few hours until we have the culture results."

"Then what?"

"He might have space by then."

"Might?"

"It's almost a guarantee," she hastened to add. "Especially after I said we'd scrub Sam clean. Oh, and by the way, Will says if he gets in trouble, he's dragging you along with him."

Trey seemed unconcerned. "Sure, why not?"

"You aren't worried?"

He grinned. "I didn't earn top honors in debate for nothing. I can hold my own."

Of course he could. The man had fine-tuned the art of persuasion. She wondered why he hadn't become a lawyer.

"The question is, can we tie up a bed in Emergency for another six hours?" she asked.

"We don't have any choice, do we?"

"No."

"Then we'll do what we do best. We wait."

Sierra didn't want to think about what might happen if Will reneged in the meantime, but if he did, they'd deal with it. Trey probably had several other options in mind, just in case.

"Out of curiosity, what would you have done if Will had refused outright?" she wanted to know.

He grinned. "Why? Were you afraid I'd go upstairs and punch him in the nose?"

The picture he'd painted made her laugh. "Afraid? No. Hoping is more like it, although you must admit he could have been more of a jerk than he was. Seriously, though. What were you going to do?"

"The same thing we're doing now. Hold Sam here in Emergency, pump him full of antibiotics and hope for Will to develop a conscience. After that, I would have made an appointment for Sam at the clinic and done my best to convince him to keep it."

"We still may have to do that," she warned.

"I know, but let's cross our fingers for Plan A to work."

"Meanwhile, I'll check with our social worker at the outpatient clinic. She may have a few suggestions on places where Sam could stay, other than a park bench."

He rose. "Thanks, Sierra."

"Don't thank me yet," she warned. "Wait until he's resting comfortably in a bed on the fifth floor."

"You'll work something out," he predicted. "I have faith in you."

As he walked away to give the news to Sam, Sierra hoped she'd live up to his belief in her.

The hours passed quickly, as they always did when one was busy. Unfortunately, according to the social worker, the halfway houses she'd contacted were full, as were the nearest relief missions.

Midafternoon, Sierra checked the computer for any preliminary culture reports. She was staring at the screen when Trey slipped into the chair beside her.

"Any news?" he demanded.

She turned the monitor so he could read the page for himself. "No growth at six hours," she said.

He sighed. "I suppose it would be tacky to wish they'd found a bug."

"It would," she agreed. "As bad a positive blood culture would be for Sam, it would certainly have made our life easier." She reached for the phone.

"What are you doing?"

She punched in four numbers. "We've followed Will's instructions to the letter and now I want to be certain he hasn't forgotten us."

Sierra fell silent, listening to the phone ring. "Will," she said brightly as soon as he answered.

His immediate curse word suggested that he wasn't happy

to hear from her, but she pressed on. "Can I send our patient to you now?"

He muttered another curse word—one more unflattering than the one before. "You wouldn't believe what I've dealt with today. I've had three codes, two diabetic crises and a case of encephalitis who has seizures every time I turn around. I won't bore you with the sundry other problems I'm trying to treat but I assure you, I'm not spending my day on sore throats and runny noses, so pardon me for making you wait five minutes longer than you'd expected."

"We're seeing a lot of people with problems, too." She clutched the receiver in a white-knuckled grip, glad for the distance between them because the temptation to poke him was strong. "Contrary to what you might think, we're not throwing parties down here for lack of anything else to do."

"I don't suppose you've changed your mind about referring him to the clinic?"

"We haven't." She hoped flattery would cure his sudden reluctance. "Besides, he needs your expertise. You're the best infectious-disease guy on staff."

"Okay, fine. Send him up in thirty minutes. And not one minute before."

She replaced the receiver with a huff of her own.

"Trouble?" Trey asked.

"No. Will's just being a jerk. We can send Sam upstairs in half an hour, but not one minute before." She folded her arms. "I'm still trying to decide if his obnoxiousness comes naturally or if he has to work at it."

Trey laughed. "It's a little of both, but who cares? He's taking Sam. Score one for Emergency."

"Yeah, but I have this feeling he's going to hold this over our heads," she warned. "He doesn't like to bend the rules and, technically, he is."

He leaned over to lightly tap her nose. "You, my dear Dr. McAllaster, worry too much. Shall we give our patient the good news?"

Trey strolled into Sam's room with Sierra beside him. The grizzly-looking fellow had been transformed into a completely different man. His beard was neatly trimmed, his graying hair was combed and several months of grime had been scrubbed from his body. Apparently worn out by the effort it had taken to make him presentable, he was snoring gently in his bed. The counter beside him held a cafeteria tray and every plate, bowl and saucer appeared as if they had been licked clean.

Trey glanced at the bag of IV fluid and noted it was nearly empty. They'd replace it before they turned him over to Madison, he decided. Considering how his colleague was going against his better judgment, Trey wouldn't give the man any cause for complaint.

As if sensing he had visitors, Sam woke with a start and rubbed his face. "Guess I dozed off," he said sheepishly. "You folks have some good beds."

"We do," Trey answered. "However, the one waiting for you upstairs is even better."

"Better? You're sending me away?"

"Just to the fifth floor," Sierra reassured him. "Dr. Madison is wonderful at treating infections like yours."

"I don't get to keep you as my doctor?" Sam cast a pointed glance at Trey.

"I work strictly in Emergency," Trey answered, flattered by Sam's trust, "but the doctors throughout our entire hospital are top-notch. You don't have to worry about a thing."

Sam frowned, clearly not liking this sudden turn of events. "If it's all the same to you, I'll be goin'."

Trey exchanged a brief glance with Sierra. "I know this is a big place, but I wouldn't advise leaving. The best way to treat your infection is with an IV, which means a few nights' stay in the hospital."

Sam shook his head. "Nope. Some of my buddies checked in here, and they never came back. Can't risk it." His voice was flat, his eyes lifeless.

"If you don't stay," Trey warned, "you may become so sick

we can't help you. Your condition isn't something to ignore or to treat lightly. Dr. McAllaster and I definitely do not want you to end up like your friends."

"Appreciate your concern, Doc, but I'm leaving. If you'll give me some pills, I'll be on my way."

Trey wasn't ready to give up. "Someone has to change the dressings on your legs every day. Will you let me schedule an appointment for you at our clinic?"

Sam's eyes narrowed. "Do I know anybody there?"

"You might." Sierra's voice was upbeat. "Even if you don't, the staff is friendly and will take care of you."

"I'd rather come back here. Unless you're tellin' me I can't."

Trey didn't want the man to think he wasn't welcome. Rumors like those never seemed to fade away. "I'm not saying you can't come back," he objected, "but we're only trying to do what's best for you. You won't have nearly as long a wait at the clinic as you do here. As you know, if we're busy—"

"Waitin' don't bother me." Sam shrugged. "Nothin' else to do."

"Are you absolutely certain we can't convince you to spend a few days with us?" Trey pressed. "A good bed, television, plenty of hot food. All the creature comforts would be here, at your fingertips."

"Naw. I've heard people pick up nasty diseases in places like this. Saw a show about it on TV. Don't want any of that. 'Sides, you're my doctor. No one else."

"I appreciate your confidence, but coming every day to the E.R. isn't your best option," Trey tried again.

"It's what I want to do." Sam's jaw was set. "If you won't see me, then I'll muddle through the best I can."

If the situation hadn't been so dire, Trey might have been amused by Sam's stubbornness over what Trey considered a minor risk. Sensing he was wasting his time, he looked at Sierra and shrugged his shoulders. Some battles just weren't worth fighting.

"Okay, but tomorrow will be a repeat of today," Trey

warned. "The IV antibiotics, the lab work, the works. And not just tomorrow, but every day until I say otherwise."

The hopeful light in Sam's eyes returned. In spite of his objections, he truly seemed to want to get better. "I'll be here."

"Because we'll see you daily, we'll dole out your pills as needed," Sierra added. "So you don't accidentally lose them."

Knowing how Sam might end up selling his medication to meet his needs, he gave Sierra a mental point for realizing it and addressing the possibility tactfully.

"I guess that'd be all right," Sam said, stroking his chin.

"Then it's settled," Trey said, not particularly happy the situation hadn't turned out the way he'd wanted, but at least Sam would receive treatment. "We'll see you in the morning, and in the meantime keep your bandages dry and clean."

"Yeah, I promise."

"Where will you go?" Sierra asked, clearly bothered by Sam's decision to leave.

"This time of year, the parks."

"Which ones?" she asked.

He guffawed. "You thinking to visit me, Doc?"

She grinned. "Don't you want me to stop and say hello? The parks are beautiful this time of year."

"Much as I'd be honored, I don't think my buddies would appreciate havin' the company. We found ourselves a few spots where we're not bothered."

"Who bothers you?" she asked.

"Cops. Other folks like me. Sometimes gangs of kids with too much time on their hands, looking for trouble. People in general. But don't worry. I know how to take care o' myself. Appreciate the thought, though."

"Do you need anything for tonight?" Trey asked. "Food? A blanket?"

"Naw, I'm good. Although if there's another one of them sandwiches like I had earlier, I'd enjoy eatin' that tonight. And maybe one for a couple of my friends who don't have much. Gettin' fresh food instead of out of a Dumpster is a real treat."

Trey couldn't imagine how anyone could be less fortunate than Sam. He might be a derelict in the world's eyes, but his willingness to share what he had was humbling.

"Done," Trey promised. "As soon as the bag is empty." He motioned toward the IV pole. "Billie will unhook you and you're free to go. Remember, we expect to see you tomorrow morning, bright and early."

"Sure thing, Doc. Thanks for ever'thing."

Outside Sam's room, Sierra met Trey's gaze. "I feel terrible. We should have forced him to stay."

"How? People have the option to accept treatment or not. Besides, you heard his reasons. We weren't going to convince him otherwise. It's a sobering fact that some people who come here don't go home."

"I only hope this plan works. I can't imagine your boss will be happy we're using this department as a walk-in clinic."

"That's why we document everything. There is a bright side to this, though."

"What?"

He grinned. "We won't owe Madison a favor after all."

Sierra phoned Will and broke the news that their patient had declined a hospital stay. He was delighted, which only irritated her for reasons she couldn't quite define.

In fact, she didn't know who she was irritated with the most—Will for rejoicing because he had one less patient, Sam for being too stubborn for his own good, or Trey for not being silver-tongued enough to change Sam's mind.

A short time later, Billie redeemed him without realizing it.

Sierra saw her walking down the hallway toward Sam's room with a large paper sack. "Did the cafeteria send over the sandwiches for Sam?"

Billie looked at her oddly. "The cafeteria doesn't deliver food to Emergency. Other than orange juice, gelatin or pudding, that is."

"Really? I saw the tray in his room earlier."

"Dr. Donovan asked me to pick up a meal for him on my way back from lunch."

She hadn't expected that. "He did? And the food in your sack?"

"Dr. Donovan gave me money to buy sandwiches, fresh fruit and vegetables."

Something shifted in her chest. "Does he send food home with his patients often?"

Billie smiled. "Define 'often.' He isn't this generous with every down-and-out person who comes in, but he helps out a good share of them."

"I'm...amazed."

Billie nodded. "He's more than just a pretty face. The woman who realizes that will be one lucky gal."

Sierra slowly made her way back to the nurses' station. Billie's revelation had been unexpected, and yet it wasn't. Trey sincerely cared about people—his staff and his patients.

Any lingering doubts about Trey vanished. In fact, hearing of one more instance of his generosity made her feel ashamed for projecting David's failings and faults onto a man who obviously didn't deserve them.

The funny thing was, during her lonely nights in her apartment she'd envisioned herself with a shy, quiet man who didn't turn heads but was a boring, steady sort she could depend on. Instead, she was falling for a guy who wasn't shy or quiet, who drew admiring glances without trying and was anything but boring. As for being steady and dependable, Trey met that criterion easily. Any man who would take care of his niece without complaint was a keeper, indeed.

"Solving the problems of the world?" Trey's voice broke into her thoughts.

"What?"

"You looked as if you were solving the problems of the world."

She dodged his hint. "Just thinking and wondering. You were going to tell me about Hannah," she reminded him.

"I'm saving my news for dinner conversation," he said.

His roundabout invitation caught her off guard. While she'd hoped they could repeat last night's experience, she hadn't expected the suggestion so soon. "You want to go out again?"

He shrugged. "Why not? We both enjoyed ourselves, didn't we?"

She nodded, eager to spend several hours with him away from the demands of the hospital but reluctant to seem *over-* eager. "What did you have in mind?"

"Do you like surprises?" he countered.

"Occasionally."

"Then prepare to be surprised."

"I didn't expect this," Sierra told Trey after he'd spread a blanket under a shade tree in Mellon Park. "I'm so glad you thought of a picnic."

"I didn't know for certain if you'd like one or not," he confessed, "but anyone who spends as many lunch hours and coffee breaks as you do in the labyrinth and hospital garden has to enjoy dining outdoors." He poured white wine into the long-stemmed glasses he'd brought.

"I didn't think anyone noticed where I went."

"People notice all sorts of things," he said, eyeing her with male approval. He'd definitely seen how her jeans fit her body and how her rose-pink tank top clung to the most delightful curves. He'd like nothing more than to caress the soft skin of her bare arms before he traced his way across her collarbone and down the creamy skin of her chest.

Those thoughts confirmed his decision to be outdoors. Being in full view of everyone was supposed to suppress his own roaring testosterone. He could have arranged for a quiet, intimate evening at his house where he could wine and dine her with elegant French food and soft music, but he'd quickly nixed the idea. It hinted at a planned seduction and knowing how Sierra considered his charm a strike against him, he refused to lose the ground he'd already gained. While he didn't know where their relationship might head, he was determined to prove just how different he was from the idiot who'd destroyed her faith in men.

He sipped his wine as he willed his body to behave. "With your Emergency experience, didn't you realize how nosiness is one of the criteria for working in our department? Curiosity is part of our collective character."

"Ah, sort of like the adrenalin rush you all enjoy?"

He grinned. "Like that. Along with our ability to eat anything at any time, anywhere. By the way, I brought fruit, cheese, and a sandwich with avocado and some sort of sprouty things."

"Alfalfa?" she asked.

"Could be. The clerk assured me they simply, and I quote, 'made' the sandwich." He flicked at an insect crawling across the blanket. "I also invited a few ants to join us. They're already arriving."

"You managed to think of everything," she teased. "What picnic would be complete without the bugs?"

He served the food out of the basket of goodies he'd purchased at the mom-and-pop gourmet grocery store near the hospital, pleased by Sierra's obvious delight over his choices. They ate in companionable silence until most of the food was gone.

After Sierra packed up the remnants—"You cooked, so I'll do the dishes," she said—he sat with his back against the tree trunk and pulled Sierra against him. He might not be able to hold her as he'd like, given the public place, but at least he could touch her.

As soon as they were settled and sipping on refills of wine, he turned the conversation to his niece.

"I talked to my brother about Hannah," he began slowly. "He had the same initial reaction I did."

Her gaze was intent, but she didn't appear offended. Instead, she simply nodded. "I'm not surprised. When you see something every day for so long, the details no longer stand out as unusual. You simply accept your observations as the way things are and you go on."

"Although some of your comments made sense, I was inclined to dismiss everything you'd said. I went over to Mitch's house to prove you were wrong." He paused, still hardly able to believe what he'd seen, but the facts seemed undeniable.

"I wasn't wrong, was I?" she asked softly.

He drew a deep breath. "No."

"What did she do?"

"Everything you said she would. Her brownies had just come out of the oven, but she refused to eat any. They were for her dad, she'd said, not her. After I coaxed her into eating one with us, she only ate crumbs. *Crumbs!*"

"That's one of the warning signs," she said. "To cook for others while giving excuses for not eating. I assume you pointed out her techniques to her father." As he nodded, she asked, "What did your brother say then?"

"That I was overreacting. That I'm seeing problems where none exist."

She nodded, as if unsurprised by his report.

"Did you get the same reaction when you told your parents about your sister?"

"To some degree," she admitted. "They were already suspicious about Leann's weight loss, but after I printed a ton of information from various internet sites, they knew I was right."

"Mitch isn't convinced Hannah doesn't eat properly, but he agreed to watch her, so I have to take some comfort in that. I hope it won't take a crisis for him to see the truth."

"As physicians, we're used to taking charge, analyzing the facts and making decisions," she said softly. "It isn't easy to sit back and watch our family members make bad choices."

"Tell me about it," he answered darkly, grateful that Sierra could relate to his circumstances.

"The question is," she asked softly, "what will you do if

you decide Hannah has an eating disorder and your brother doesn't support you?"

"I'm hoping it won't come to that, but if it does, I'll intervene. For Hannah's sake, I'll have to," he said simply, "even if it means causing a rift between us. With luck, he'll see what we've seen. Then I'll help him deal with it."

"Have you always been his Rock of Gibraltar?"

His chuckle was weak. "Are you kidding? I was the younger brother and *he* was the one who loved to dispense free advice. After Marcy died, I fell into his role as the older, wiser sibling out of necessity."

"Necessity? What happened?"

He thought for a moment. "I don't believe Mitch ever expected Marcy to die. He had so much faith in medicine curing her that when it didn't, he was crushed."

"We can cure so many diseases we couldn't before, it becomes easy to think we can prescribe a pill for everything," she said wryly. "Unfortunately, research and modern science can't always do that."

"Yeah. For the next few weeks after the funeral, 'numb' was the best way to describe Mitch. Half the time he forgot to eat, take a shower, change clothes or go to work. Someone had to take charge of Hannah, so I went by every night after work and made sure she had food, clean clothes, the works. Marcy's sister offered to take her, but if Mitch didn't have Hannah to live for, I was afraid he'd never pull himself together. So I convinced him to keep her and promised to do everything I could to help."

"Your plan obviously worked," she commented.

"To a point," Trey admitted. "Eventually, he started drinking. After I discovered he was coping through alcohol—and not just an occasional drink—I threatened to take Hannah away from him if he didn't stop. That same day, he hit rock bottom."

"What happened?"

"He didn't pick up Hannah from school. She hung around the playground until eight o'clock at night—this was in

November, so it was cold and dark—before she walked to a neighborhood convenience store and called me."

"She didn't call her father?"

"Mitch didn't answer," he explained. "Anyway, I drove over and got her and we went by their house. Mitch was at home, passed out on the sofa. Hannah spent the next few nights with me, and two days later, after he sobered up, I gave him an ultimatum—if he didn't enter a treatment program, I'd commit him myself and file for custody of Hannah. Mitch went. And Hannah has carried a cell phone ever since."

"Did she attend any counseling sessions at the time?"

"She went for a while, but her therapist said she was handling the stress well for a child her age. Hindsight tells me she wasn't dealing with her emotional turmoil as well as we all thought," he finished wryly.

"You won't know for certain until she sees someone who specializes in eating disorders."

He agreed, but getting Hannah to the right person wouldn't be easy. "It's tough, being in my position," he admitted. "I don't have any authority to do what's best. All I can do is give advice when I'd rather take charge myself." He paused. "Actually, that isn't entirely true. I'd rather have my older brother back—the one who had an answer for everything. The one who loved to boss me around because he was a year older." He smiled, remembering. "Back then, I was the irresponsible younger brother. My footloose lifestyle drove him crazy."

"I'll bet it did," she said. "I'll also bet that deep down he hates having to depend on you."

He thought about how short-tempered Mitch had been when he'd mentioned Hanna's eating habits. "If it's true," he said slowly, "then those feelings should give him the impetus to change."

"He might not know where to begin. Maybe he doesn't have the confidence to try. I certainly understand what you're going through," she said thoughtfully, as if recalling her own experiences. "You can only do so much and after that you feel helpless."

"Exactly."

"And I sympathize with you on the tightrope you're walking. If you push him too hard, he could cut you out of his life, and you wouldn't want that to happen."

"I can't imagine what I'd do without Hannah," he admitted. "Which is why I'll give him a few days for everything I've told him to sink in. After that, I'll do whatever's necessary for Hannah's well-being."

"If you think it would help, I'd be happy to talk to Mitch," she offered. "To Hannah, too."

The idea of involving another person in his family's problems was somewhat unsettling, although at the same time it felt good to have another person's viewpoint. "You don't think I can handle it?" he teased.

"I think you can talk anyone into anything," she answered back with a smile. "I only offered because she may feel more comfortable about sharing her thoughts with me than with you or with her father."

He hugged her, enjoying the feel of her smooth skin as he breathed in her citrusy scent. "You are a smart, intuitive woman, Dr. McAllaster."

"Why, thank you, Dr. D." As she smiled at him, he had the sudden urge to kiss her. He didn't know how the evening would end, but if the opportunity presented itself, he wouldn't run away from her like he had before. "Then you'll let me talk to Hannah?"

"If Mitch doesn't cooperate by Friday, yes."

"Your brother is lucky you're watching his back. A lot of people in his situation don't have that luxury."

"What can I say?" He shrugged. "We're family."

CHAPTER EIGHT

IN SPITE of the problems Trey was embroiled in, Sierra was jealous of his relationship with his brother and niece. Before she could voice it, the sky clouded over and a light drizzle began to fall.

"Picnic's over," he announced cheerfully as he pulled Sierra to her feet. They took off across the lawn just as the heavens opened and the rain fell in earnest.

"Head for the gazebo," Trey yelled.

By the time they reached the structure, they were both soaked. Rivulets of water ran down his face and his hair was plastered to his head. His clothes were wet and his cotton shirt was now transparent enough to reveal the shadow of chest hair underneath.

He might appear bedraggled, but he still oozed masculinity. She, on the other hand, probably looked a fright.

"I hope you didn't order the rain on my account," she commented as she wrung out her hair.

"It came as part of my surprise package." He guided her toward the center of the structure. "Sit here. Less splashing."

Sierra waited as he positioned the blanket. The rain poured off the roof in sheets, creating a curtain of privacy, just as it had the other night while they'd been in his car.

She shivered, as much from awareness as from being wet, and quickly rubbed at the goose bumps forming on her bare arms. "We're lucky we stumbled across this place. We would have ruined your leather upholstery if we'd tried to dash to the car."

"Yeah, this is much nicer. Have a seat." He patted a spot on the floor beside him. "You look cold."

"Just a little," she said as she obeyed. He drew her close then pulled the blanket's free edge over their shoulders until they were both cocooned in its warmth.

Trey's body heat felt wonderful against her chilled skin and she soaked it up like a sponge. Before long, her shivers stopped.

"Better?" he asked.

"Much," she said as she snuggled against him. "I must say, though, you certainly know how to show a girl a good time."

He chuckled. "I aim to please. I can break out the wine and cheese again if you'd like."

"Thanks, but I'm stuffed. More wine will only make me sleepy." She stifled a yawn.

"In that case, let's get more comfortable."

Before she knew it, he'd spread out the blanket and they were lying flat on the floor. He'd tucked her under his arm, offering his shoulder as a pillow.

"Now I really will go to sleep," she said as she enjoyed the sensation of his rock-hard body against hers.

"There's not a lot we can do while we're waiting for the rain to let up," he said. "Feel free."

She fingered a button on his shirt, thinking of several things they could do—several things that would create a public-relations nightmare for Good Shepherd if two of their Emergency physicians were caught doing them.

"We could play 'I spy.'"

"Considering how we can't see past a few feet, we're a little limited, wouldn't you say?" he asked. "Too bad I didn't pack a deck of cards."

Sierra thought for a moment. "When we traveled as kids, my mother would always play word games with us. We'd take turns saying words that began with each letter of the alphabet."

"Apple," he said promptly.

She swatted him playfully as she noticed his hair had turned from dripping wet to damp. "No, silly. We're going to make this more challenging. We have to use medical terms."

"Medical words, eh?"

"Yes. I'll start. Alopecia."

He flipped her onto her back. "Are you implying I'm turning bald?" he asked in a mock growl.

She raised her hand to run her fingers through the now-curling strands. "Absolutely not. You have thick, beautiful hair. Your turn."

"*B*. Let me see. There's so many to choose from. Brain." He touched her head. "Bronchiole." He spread his hand across her chest before his gaze grew intent and his voice soft. "Breast." His fingers slowly outlined her shape.

Oh, my. "You only have to name one," she said, suddenly breathless.

"Okay." He smiled widely as he moved his hand to safer territory. "Bunion."

She giggled at his choice. Considering where his hand had roamed, she hadn't expected *bunion*.

"*C* to you," he reminded her as he brushed a strand of hair off her face.

The sparks flying were so powerful she could hardly think as she stared into his face. Unbidden, her hands inched upward until they rested on his shoulders.

"Giving up?" he teased. "How about—?"

She noticed a tiny scar near his nose which might have been left over from a childhood disease. "Chicken pox," she blurted.

He clicked his tongue. "The correct medical term is varicella. Don't you want to save it for your *V* word?"

"I planned to use *vasectomy*."

He winced. "Ouch. Okay, my turn. Deltoid." This time,

he trailed his fingers along the muscle covering her shoulder joint.

"Effleurage." As he caressed her arm, it only seemed natural to think of the massage procedure that increased blood flow and reduced swelling.

He grabbed her hand and pulled her fingers to his mouth. "Fingerprint," he murmured.

It was a very sensual experience to feel his full lips with her fingers. "That is definitely not a medical word."

"Why not?" he asked innocently. "Fingerprint patterns can show the presence of inherited diseases. Don't tell me you've forgotten about dermatoglyphics."

At this point, she had almost forgotten her own name.

"My answer isn't any worse than *chicken pox*," he pointed out.

"All right. We'll let it pass. Where are we?"

"*G.*"

"Ganglion."

"Hormone."

At the moment, her body was pumping out estrogen fast and furiously. "Intubation."

"Jaw." He released her hand to stroke her jawline with the back of his hand.

She swallowed hard and forced herself to concentrate on words instead of the sensations he was creating in her body. "Kernicterus."

"For the letter *K,* I have one better."

"You don't like my word for brain damage caused by hemolytic disease of the newborn? Is it too medical for you?" she teased.

"Nope. Too depressing. My word is *kiss of life.*"

His head lowered until she felt his breath caress her cheek. His scent surrounded her and his mouth hovered dangerously close. "You're referring to artificial respiration, I presume?"

"We're on the letter *K,* which means my phrase meets

all the game requirements, and then some." The distance between them instantly disappeared and he kissed her.

To say the earth moved would be an understatement, but it was the best description Sierra could give. Shirt buttons came undone, clasps were unhooked and skin met skin as the rain poured and thunder rumbled.

At one point, she found herself on top of him, their legs intertwined as he greedily nibbled his way across her collarbone before turning south at the hollow of her throat.

Her own hands frantically traced his hard ridges as each caress only made her want more.

Slowly, gradually, the frantic quality faded, but the electricity they'd generated still sparked the air.

"The rain's stopping," he commented as he held her on top of him.

She opened her eyes and listened. Water no longer cascaded off the roof in sheets and the drops hitting the roof sounded like musical chimes instead of drumbeats.

The privacy the rain had afforded them was gone.

"So it is," she said, trying to hide her disappointment.

"Don't look so sad," he said as he kissed her nose. "Be glad."

He was *happy* their romantic interlude had come to an end? "Excuse me?"

Before she could work up a good case of embarrassment and anger, he rolled onto his side, taking her with him. "The floor is killing my back," he said. "Now we can take this someplace far more comfortable."

He wanted to…*continue?*

He chuckled at her expression. "You'll catch flies like that," he said as he sat up, readjusted her clothing as if she were a child, then stood.

She watched him button his shirt as everything from astonishment to excitement flooded over her until she didn't know what to do, say or think.

He paused, suddenly appearing uncertain. "Unless you don't want to go someplace more private?"

"Oh, no. That's not it at all," she reassured him. "I'm just... surprised, I guess."

He took a step forward and slid his arms around her waist. "Are you really? This has been building between us for a long time. Wouldn't you agree?"

"Yes," she said faintly, "but—"

"Am I moving too fast? Your husband hasn't been gone very long—"

"This doesn't have anything to do with him. I'm sad to say our marriage had ended quite a while before he died."

He brushed another kiss against her lips. "Then the only question now is...your place or mine?"

Her heart seemed to pound right out of her chest. "I do still owe you a cup of coffee."

"Your place it is," he said, sounding satisfied. "Grab the blanket and let's go before it starts raining again."

"You don't want to stay here?" She cast one last glance around the gazebo as Trey exited the structure. As far as she was concerned, it possessed a magic she hadn't expected to find tonight.

He beckoned her through the doorway, his grin positively feral. "Not for what I have in mind."

The drive to Sierra's home took thirty minutes, but it seemed like an hour.

She couldn't believe she'd invited a man home with her—much less one who represented everything she'd rejected—but she had. Neither could she believe how difficult it was to hold on to her control, especially as they drew closer to her front door.

"Decaf or regular?" she asked as soon as they were inside her apartment.

"I'll have the high-octane stuff," he said as he took her into his arms.

"Really? Hannah says you won't sleep—"

"I'm not planning on sleeping anytime soon. Are you?"

After that, she remembered nothing, and everything.

Somehow the door closed, somehow her clothes littered the floor and his followed, and somehow she found herself in her bedroom, lying against the comforter and downy pillows, staring into the face of the man she was growing to love against her better judgment.

He touched her as if trying to memorize every inch, and every caress was a torment designed to drive her wild. His body fit against hers perfectly and she eventually lost the sensation of being separate. After a pause, one just long enough to make sure they were safe from future repercussions, he was inside her.

She welcomed him, wrapping her arms around him as tightly as he held her. He whispered sweet words in her ear—gentle words that were so beautiful and so poignant she wanted to cry.

When her body shattered and pure pleasure exploded, she trembled in his embrace and wept from sheer happiness. The power in that room amazed her to the point where she couldn't begin to talk about what had taken place. She could only marvel at how fate had been kind enough to grant her this boon—to experience lovemaking in a way she'd never experienced before.

It was exactly what she was doing—loving a man with her body as much as she loved him with her soul. How she'd arrived at this point, she wasn't sure. She only knew that her feelings had crept on her gradually, with one building on another until the final product couldn't be described in any other way.

They lay with their arms and legs intertwined as raindrops struck the windows and an occasional burst of thunder punctuated the near-quiet. Her body cooled and her breathing slowed, just as his did. The rapid thump of his heart steadied under her hand and she felt his muscles relax.

She was exhausted. She was sated. She was…pleased beyond everything she'd ever imagined. As she lay limply against him, she wondered if his experience had matched hers. For her, making love had never been this potent, this cataclysmic, but it wasn't fair to compare David to Trey. The event that had taken place had been too beautiful to destroy it with pointless comparisons. David had been her past and it was best to leave him there.

Trey, however, could be her future. She hoped so.

Never say never.

He nuzzled her neck. "You're wonderful."

"I'll bet you say that—" She cut herself off. She had no business asking about the women he'd been with, so she switched mental gears. "You," she stressed, "are more than wonderful." She scooted up on one elbow to press her lips against his stubbled cheek. "I mean that most sincerely."

His eyes seemed to darken. "I'm thirty-six years old, Sierra, and I haven't been celibate by any means."

He'd obviously guessed at her fears and chose to address them head-on. "I didn't expect you would be," she said in a small voice.

"For the record, there haven't been as many encounters as you think."

Trey had shattered every preconceived idea, every misconception she'd had, so it wasn't surprising he would do the same with this one. "Then you aren't the self-indulgent playboy I first imagined?" she teased.

He laughed. "Thanks for putting me in my place. However, I can safely state you are an eighteen on a scale of one to ten."

While she was relieved his experience wasn't as extensive as she'd thought, she also knew this chapter in their life together had to be separate from the previous ones.

"Let's make a deal," she suggested. "I won't ask about your past loves if you don't ask about mine. What matters is us, from today on."

"Deal," he said.

She traced circles on his chest. "Are you ready for your coffee now?"

He flipped her onto her back before covering her with his body. "Maybe later. Right now, I'd rather have you."

"You've been more cheerful than normal the past few days," Roma commented to Trey on Thursday.

"Really?" he asked, feigning surprise. "I thought I was being my usual chipper self."

The head nurse cocked her head and showed him her familiar give-me-a-break expression. "I know you too well. You and Dr. McAllaster have something going, don't you?"

Her phrase didn't adequately describe what his life with Sierra had been like since the evening in the gazebo. He simply couldn't get enough of her. In fact, he was already trying to work out the logistics for when Hannah returned to his house. While he was certain she would be happy to have Sierra around, he didn't like the moral picture the action would paint. Discretion was necessary, along with a bit of creativity and a lot of self-control.

The last item would be tough because he didn't seem to have any when Sierra was around. Earlier today he'd resorted to pulling her into the on-call room for a long, drawn-out kiss because waiting until the shift ended seemed like an unfair penance. He also had to wait until they'd left the hospital before she'd take down her hair. It was definitely a good thing she kept it braided while on duty because otherwise he'd be too distracted to do his job.

"I don't kiss and tell," he said.

"Humph. Whatever. But if you aren't making her walk like she's four feet off the ground, who is?"

Trey smiled broadly. "Four feet off the ground, eh?"

"You *are* the one. I *knew* it," she crowed. "Billie wanted to start a betting pool and—"

"Please tell me you didn't," he begged. If Sierra got wind of this, she'd be mortified, not to mention furious. It would be too easy for her to believe he'd only wined and dined her because of a bet and he'd never convince her otherwise.

"Didn't start the pool or didn't bet?"

"Either. Both."

"Sorry. I picked two weeks, which, I might add, was longer than everyone else believed you'd need."

"At the risk of stating the obvious, she'd better not find out," he warned. "Or each of you will live to regret it."

She rolled her eyes. "Give us a little credit, Doc. We like her, too, you know. I don't suppose you're trying to convince her to stay, are you? If they're hiring another doctor anyway, why can't they give the floor position to the new person?"

Trey wasn't inclined to explain Sierra's reasons. The story was hers to tell. "I've mentioned it, but she prefers handling medical cases instead of traumas. You're free to try and persuade her to change her mind, though."

"I will. By the way, I haven't seen Sam today. Did you tell him he didn't have to come in anymore?"

Trey shook his head. "No, I didn't."

"Well, he's usually here by eight and now it's two in the afternoon," she said. "You don't suppose he's decided he's had enough, do you?"

"The man always leaves with a sack of groceries," he said wryly. "He wouldn't pass up free food without a compelling reason. In fact, I'm expecting him to show up daily from now on, sick or not."

"True. We're lucky he hasn't hauled in a bunch of his friends just for the goodies. If I see him, though, I'll let you know."

"Thanks."

Sierra slid into the seat Roma had vacated. "Who are you looking for?"

"Sam. He didn't show up today."

"Really? I'm surprised."

"Me, too."

"Are you worried about him?"

"A little," he admitted. "He's doing well enough that skipping a day probably won't affect his recovery, but he doesn't seem the type to break a promise. And he did promise…" His mind raced with options.

"What are you thinking?"

"Nothing," he prevaricated, simply because his idea was still forming.

"I'm not buying it," she said. "You're planning to look for him, aren't you?"

"I might," he admitted, "but the day isn't over. He might surprise us and walk in at any minute."

Unfortunately, Sam hadn't appeared by the end of their shift. Trey might have chalked up Sam's absence to chance, but his gut said otherwise, especially after he'd overheard two paramedics talking about a recent trend of gang members targeting homeless people.

He was going to cancel his dinner plans with Sierra before he left, but he couldn't find her.

"You just missed her," one of the nurses told him.

"No problem," he said. "I'll text her."

He thumbed his keypad as he walked out of the hospital, wishing he could have canceled their date in person, but it couldn't be helped. To his surprise, he saw Sierra standing on the street corner, talking to two patrolmen. An instant later, she waved at him.

So much for thinking she'd gone home… For some reason, he could read Sierra as plainly as he read an eye chart and he instinctively knew what she was doing. Or trying to do.

"Hi," she greeted him when they met halfway.

"What were you doing?"

"Talking to the police," she said cheerfully. "I asked if they knew Sam or had seen him lately."

"And?"

"He's fallen off their radar screens, too. They did tell me where he lives, though, so we can look for him."

"We?"

"Yeah, we." She smiled. "I'm going with you."

"You can't."

"Oh, please. Don't give me the 'it isn't safe' argument. You're going."

He fought for control. "Sierra, homeless people don't hang around the best parts of town."

"Sam said he stays in the parks."

"He also said he and his friends go where they aren't bothered. Considering what I heard earlier, they probably tucked themselves away so well we wouldn't notice if we walked past them. We certainly won't find them by strolling through the park on well-marked paths."

She threaded her arm through his. "Then aren't you glad you'll have company?"

Darkness was falling when Trey called a halt to their search several hours later.

"I can't believe we haven't found him," Sierra mentioned, disheartened by their failure. "I was *positive* those two men we met had more information than they were telling us."

"This is an entirely different world," he told her. "These people don't trust anyone. Even if they knew something, they wouldn't share it with people they don't know."

"Then what are we supposed to do?" she fretted.

"We wait. With any luck, those two guys will let Sam know we're looking for him. After that, it's up to Sam. We did the best we could."

"I suppose, but it still feels as if it's not enough."

"Sometimes, it isn't," he admitted, "but our hands are tied for now."

"We could call the police."

"Someone has to be missing for more than twenty-four hours before the police will act. Trust me, finding a homeless person won't land at the top of their priority list."

Sierra sighed and turned her thoughts to someone they could help. Sam might fall through the cracks of the system, but she would not let Hannah do the same. In a few short weeks the little girl had wiggled her way into Sierra's heart. She'd always wanted children even if David hadn't, and the idea of this little, motherless child struggling through life on her own was more than she could bear. If Hannah had been *her* daughter, she would have wanted some kind soul to take her under her wing.

"Have you heard anything about Hannah? Has your brother seen any of the behavior we'd mentioned?" she asked.

"I'll visit with him tomorrow," he said.

"I'm sorry for being so impatient. I just don't want this problem to drag on indefinitely. She's such a special girl—"

His gaze grew speculative. "You really like her, don't you?"

"Yeah, I do, and the sooner she gets help—"

"The better she'll be," he finished. "Yes, I know." He walked her to her door. "Now, stop worrying about Sam and about Hannah. Things always look better in the morning."

Unfortunately, Sam didn't appear the next day at their agreed-on time either. Sierra knew Trey was worried, but they were swamped with enough people who *had* come to Emergency that neither of them could dwell on the situation.

Finally, at eleven, the two men they'd talked to the night before came in, carrying Sam between them.

Sierra immediately stopped Billie. "Find Dr. Donovan, stat," she ordered, before she motioned the men into a trauma room where they placed Sam on the bed. "I see you found him," she told the two, who were as ragged as Sam had been the first time she'd seen him.

The dark-haired one nodded. "After you told us you were lookin' for Sam, we decided to do some searchin' ourselves."

"Good thing, too," the other said. "Sam was in bad shape."

Sierra cranked up the head of the bed so Sam could lean against it, taking note of the homemade splint attached to his lower leg. Before she could ask what had happened, Trey strode in.

"Sam!" he exclaimed. "We've been wondering if you forgot your appointment with us."

"Didn't forget. I couldn't make it," he said, his voice hoarse with pain. "The craziest darn thing happened. I was crossing one of the streambeds and slipped on a wet rock. I've done it a hundred, no, a *thousand* times, and never fell, till yesterday. When I landed, I busted my leg. If these guys hadn't found me, I'd still be there."

They'd used two saplings as splints, which had been a smart thing to do because the bone in his leg was crooked. Fortunately, the skin remained intact, indicating a simple rather than a compound fracture.

"After you folks came round last night, Earl and I decided somethin' was wrong," the dark-haired one interrupted, "so we spent all night lookin' for him. Found Sam early this morning, so we brought him here as quick as we could."

"You have good friends," Trey told his patient.

Sam nodded weakly. "So can you fix me up, Doc, and send me on my way?"

"You'll need an orthopedic guy." Sam visibly steeled himself to the pain as Trey ran his hands lightly over the site. "Depending on how the bone has broken, you may need surgery."

"Aw, Doc, you know I can't stay here," Sam warned him.

"We can't compromise on this," Trey was adamant.

"We gotta come up with somethin', Doc." Sam sounded frantic.

Trey hesitated. "I have an idea. Would you be willing to stick around if your brothers stayed with you? Just to keep an eye on everything."

Sam scratched his head. "Brothers? We're not—" His face suddenly lit up as he clearly understood. "Why, sure. If my *brothers* can make sure I'm taken care of, I could stay a night or two."

"Good. Then let's get some X-rays, shall we?"

Sierra shook her head in amazement. If anyone could convince the nursing staff that Sam's family background was diverse enough to allow for a black and a Hispanic brother, it would be Trey.

She patted Sam's arm. "Dr. Donovan has everything under control, so I'll be on my way."

"Thanks for tryin' to hunt me down," Sam said. "I owe you."

Being an emergency doctor was a funny thing, she decided as she headed toward her next patient. One saw humanity at its worst, but occasionally someone redeemed it by an act of kindness. Sam's two friends had definitely re-energized her faith in human nature.

Working in Emergency wasn't so bad after all, she decided. In fact, she was slowly coming to enjoy the job as much as she had before David's death. Whether she wanted to remain in this department full-time was still in question, but she'd gotten this far and she owed her progress to Trey.

Her next patient had been mowing his lawn and swore that a blade of grass was stuck in his eye. After checking to ensure nothing was present and his cornea hadn't been scratched, she prescribed antibiotic eyedrops. As she finished explaining her treatment and advised him to see his personal ophthalmologist if he continued to have problems, she received a text message.

Ambulance en route. ETA two minutes. Ten-year-old female with possible heat exhaustion.

Sierra barreled into the hallway where she ran into Trey. "Are you free?" he asked.

"Yes, but where's Marissa?"

"She's in the middle of a spinal tap. Can you handle it while I send Sam to Radiology?"

"No problem," she said without hesitation.

"See you later, then."

Sierra and Billie both raced to the ambulance-bay doors, arriving just as the paramedics wheeled in their gurney. The small figure lay motionless with her eyes closed. Her face was pale underneath the oxygen mask and her brown hair was damp at her temples.

"Ten-year-old girl collapsed at her dance class," paramedic John Evans reported. "Heartbeat is irregular and BP is ninety over forty."

Arrhythmia and hypotensive. "Get her into Trauma Five," she ordered, "and hook her up to the monitors asap. Have the parents been contacted?"

"The dance instructor was notifying her father as we were leaving," John reported as they rushed into the trauma and parked the gurney beside the bed. "According to her, she got dizzy, then fainted. The instructor tried to cool her down and get her to drink water and orange juice, but there wasn't any improvement, so she called 911.

"Shortly after we arrived, she went into cardiac arrest. She came back after we shocked her twice. She's in regular sinus rhythm now."

"Let's move her on three," Sierra said. "One, two, *three*." The four of them lifted. As Sierra turned her corner of the sheet loose, she looked down at the brown-haired girl and recognized her.

It was Hannah. Sweet, precious, Hannah.

Oh, dear. Déjà vu struck, but she brushed it aside. Hannah needed expert medical care and Sierra would see that she received it. Without hesitation, she called out her orders.

"I want basic chemistry, a CBC and a blood gas. Start another IV and get Dr. Landower in here *now*," she ordered as the nurses attached Hannah's body to the overhead monitor. Although she didn't want to call Trey in until Marissa took over, she didn't have a choice. He would never forgive her if he learned she'd delayed contacting him, even if Hannah needed an objective physician far more than she needed a frantic relative.

"Then text Dr. Donovan and ask him to come to Trauma Five as soon as he's able," she added.

"Shall I tell him…?" Billie asked, already thumbing buttons on her cell phone.

"Give him only the information I told you," she said firmly.

She didn't want him to panic and fly in before they stabilized Hannah's condition.

Fortunately, the heart monitor was beeping with regularity, but Sierra thought the signs pointed in a direction away from heatstroke—a direction that Hannah's father might struggle to accept, even though he'd been forewarned. She wouldn't know for certain until the blood samples they'd just drawn were tested.

Five minutes later, Marissa Landower walked in.

"What's going on?" the pediatrician asked in her calm, unhurried voice.

Sierra reported what the paramedics had stated, including her own observations and treatment measures. She glanced at the overhead monitor, aware of her colleague doing the same. Hannah's heartbeat remained fairly regular and while her blood pressure was still low, the numbers were higher than when she'd first arrived.

Hannah tried to brush at the mask covering her face, but Sierra grabbed her slender arm. Leaning in close, she spoke. "Hannah, it's me, Sierra. You're going to be just fine. I want you to relax while we help you feel better."

Her eyelids fluttered, but she nodded.

"Don't worry about a thing," Sierra soothed. "I'll stay with you until your uncle arrives."

"Uncle?" Marissa's gaze met Sierra's.

Sierra nodded. "Hannah is Trey's niece."

"Where is he?" she asked.

"Right here," he said cheerfully as he strode into the room. "What can I do?"

Sierra exchanged a glance with Marissa. Knowing Hannah was in excellent hands, she stepped away from the bedside to grab Trey's arm and pull him towards the door. "Nothing at the moment."

"Then why the stat message?"

"Trey," she said softly, hoping he'd see the concern in her eyes, "it's Hannah."

"Hannah?" he asked dumbly. "*My* Hannah?"

She nodded. "I'm afraid so."

CHAPTER NINE

"At the moment, she's stable," Sierra told Trey, eager to reassure him so he'd lose his deer-in-the-headlights look. "But her heart had stopped on the way in. Paramedics had to defibrillate."

"No." His face blanched and he tried to walk forward, but only made it two steps. He was shaking so badly he grabbed hold of the bedside table and held on with a white-knuckled grip. "No," he repeated.

Everyone looked stricken and busied themselves with their tasks to give him a minute to compose himself. Sierra knew better than most how he felt—how suddenly it became too difficult to breathe because shock had driven all the air out of one's lungs.

"She's better, Trey," she said gently, touching his arm. "See the monitor? She hasn't left us."

"Is she taking any medication, Trey?" Marissa asked.

He shook his head. "Nothing. She's always been healthy."

Before her eyes, he straightened and squared his shoulders before forcing his way past Sierra to ease up against the bed. "Hannah? Honey, it's me. Uncle Trey."

"Hi, Uncle Trey," the little girl said weakly. "I didn't mean...to be a bother."

He stroked her forehead. "You'll never be a bother," he told her tenderly. "Just rest for now. We'll have you feeling better soon."

"Okay. Next time, I promise I'll drink more water before I go to class." She closed her eyes.

"I have her labs," a nurse reported as she came in. As she recited the figures, Sierra's heart sank. Hannah's electrolytes were terrible and her blood gas reflected a ketoacidotic state that reflected problems in carbohydrate metabolism. Contrary to what the little girl thought, more water wouldn't have helped.

Marissa frowned as she looked at Trey. "This doesn't make sense," she said. "I'd expected to see different symptoms. Is she a diabetic?"

The picture was undeniable. Sierra challenged Trey with her gaze and waited expectantly for his answer.

"She may be anorexic," he said hoarsely.

The other woman's eyes widened. "Now, *that*," she said with certainty, "makes sense. As soon as I'm satisfied she's stable, I'll send her to Peds. When she's out of danger, we'll arrange for her to enter the eating-disorders unit. Do you want to tell her father, or shall I?"

"I'll talk to him," he said. "We'll meet you upstairs."

"Fair enough."

When he didn't move, Sierra took his arm and tugged him toward the doorway. He resisted at first then followed her out of the trauma room. "Let's find Mitch," she said.

He nodded, obviously too lost in his own thoughts to object.

Sierra came across Mitch Donovan as he paced the hallway outside the waiting room. The resemblance between Trey and Mitch was striking. "Mr. Donovan—Mitch," she said, extending a hand, "Sierra McAllaster. I took care of Hannah when the paramedics first brought her into Emergency."

"How is she?"

"She's much better, but she isn't out of danger yet."

"Was it heat exhaustion, like they said?" he asked.

She glanced at Trey, whose face was stony. "No," she said. "What we saw are complications of anorexia. I believe Trey has talked to you about our suspicions?"

Mitch sank onto the nearest chair. "He said, but I didn't… I watched her, I really did," he defended, "and she ate. A little," he amended. "No less than usual."

"Did she vomit after she left the table?"

He shrugged. "I don't know. If this is what she's doing, I don't understand why."

"Dr. Landower will arrange for her to see someone who specializes in eating disorders," she said gently. "They'll work with your family to help her overcome this."

"This makes no sense," he muttered. "Wouldn't she be depressed or something? She always seems so happy…"

"At this point, we can only speculate about what's going on in Hannah's head, but Good Shepherd has wonderful therapists who will help your family sort it out."

Mitch looked at Trey. "I want another opinion," he demanded. "My little girl wouldn't starve herself on purpose."

"Dr. Landower, our pediatrician, agrees with us." Trey spoke grimly and with authority. "How many more doctors have to agree before you admit Hannah has a problem?"

"We can't ignore what just happened," Sierra added. "Whatever her issues are, she won't resolve them on her own. She'll get worse. She could even die."

"Die?" Mitch's color fled and he pinched the bridge of his nose. "Okay. We'll do whatever you say. Can I see her?"

"They'll be taking her upstairs to a room shortly, so you can go along."

She accompanied both men to Hannah's trauma room. Mitch went inside to be with his daughter and Trey hesitated in the hallway. "I never truly understood what you went through with your husband, until now. The sinking feeling you get is indescribable."

"It is," she admitted. "I'm sorry you had to experience it. It's hard to see someone we love strapped to a gurney in critical condition. There's a reason we don't treat family members. But she's going to be fine, so concentrate on that."

He nodded. "I will." Apparently unconcerned about potential spectators, he tipped up her chin and kissed her gently. "Thanks, Sierra. I'll see you later."

"Later" came the next morning, when Trey reported for duty. On the surface, he appeared as impeccably groomed as always, but Sierra saw his underlying exhaustion. He obviously hadn't slept very well, if at all. While he was polite, he had little to say and no one pressed him. Word had spread of Hannah's condition and everyone trod lightly around him. When he announced his plans to skip out after lunch for their first family meeting with Hannah's treatment in the eating-disorders unit, no one objected.

Sierra had expected him to return to Emergency in an hour, but the hour stretched to two, then three.

"I hope nothing is wrong," Roma fretted.

"Me, too. I suspect the first meeting took longer than they'd expected—first meetings often do—and he probably decided it was too late to bother coming back."

"Probably," Roma agreed, but she didn't appear completely convinced. "We'll see him tomorrow."

"I'm sure we will."

Sierra didn't feel like waiting until then. She found Hannah's room—room 544, which was close to her old stomping ground—and poked her nose inside, expecting to see Trey or Mitch, or both. She saw neither. Hannah, however, saw her.

"Hi, sweetie," she said as she stroked the little girl's forehead. "How are you feeling?"

"Okay, I guess."

Hannah's gaze darted around the room and she picked at the sheet covering her. Her restless movements didn't escape Sierra's notice.

She grabbed Hannah's hand. "Are you scared?"

Hannah bit her lip and didn't answer. Finally, she nodded ever so slightly.

"It's frightening when our secrets aren't secrets anymore."

"But they aren't bad when they don't hurt anyone," Hannah blurted. "My dad said so."

"Your secret *was* hurting someone," Sierra said. "It was hurting *you*."

"But why did they have to tell him?" she wailed. "He didn't have to know. It could have stayed between you and me and Uncle Trey."

"Sweetheart, your dad *needs* to know, because he's your father. He loves you very much."

"I'm not sure he does," she said, brushing at her red-rimmed eyes. "He loved my mom and was home every night to watch her practice her dancing. After she died, he started staying away. If he really loved me, he'd come home, too."

Anger rose inside Sierra. Anger at the obviously incompetent therapist this family had seen so long ago—the same therapist who'd said that Hannah had adjusted to the stress in her life so well.

"It may seem like he doesn't, but he does love you, Hannah. Sometimes it's hard for a guy to show it."

The little girl nodded. "That's why—" She stopped abruptly, pulled her hand out of Sierra's grip and fisted the sheet.

"Why what?" Sierra coaxed. "Is that why you stopped eating? So he'd come home every night?"

"I thought if I could be more like my mom and dance the way she did, he'd love me and smile again. And maybe he wouldn't miss her so much."

This time, Sierra pulled the child into her arms. "Oh, Hannah. It isn't your job to make your dad happy. He has to figure out how to feel better for himself."

He had, she realized. According to Trey, Mitch had found his happiness in a bottle, which had only spurred Hannah to work harder at her own plan. They were stuck in a vicious circle while Trey was running alongside, trying to break them free. Thank goodness he now had support because, with Hannah being a minor, family counseling would be required.

For the first time since she'd realized Hannah had a problem, she breathed easier. Their story wouldn't end on a tragic note.

Hannah pulled away. "Will they still let me dance?" she asked in a small voice.

"If dancing makes you happy, I don't see why anyone would stop you," she answered. "The key will be learning how to balance doing the thing you love with your eating habits. There are so many people who want you to succeed, Hannah, so don't be afraid to ask for help from your dad, your uncle, the people here at the hospital—"

"You?" Hannah asked, her beautiful eyes hopeful.

"And, yes, me. I'm never more than a phone call or a text message away." Sierra rose. "Now, you should get some rest."

"Do you know where my dad or Uncle Trey are?" she asked. "They left *hours* ago and haven't come back."

"I'll ask the nurse for you," Sierra said, but she'd only taken a step toward the door when Mitch walked in. A very haggard-looking Mitch.

"Daddy!" Hannah exclaimed. "I've been waiting and waiting and *waiting* for you."

"Sorry, hon. Our meeting lasted longer than I expected." He bent down to kiss his daughter on her forehead. "How are you?"

"Better, now that you're here," she said. "Where's Uncle Trey?"

"He went home to take a nap," Mitch said smoothly. "He'll stop by later to visit."

As she said her goodbyes and saw Mitch sink tiredly into the bedside chair, she wondered about Trey. The meeting had obviously been emotionally draining for Mitch to appear so exhausted. How had Trey fared? Hannah and her father could lean on each other, but who did Trey lean on?

Suddenly, Sierra wished for nothing more than to be an official part of this group. Because she could relate to their problems, they seemed like hers, too. She would dearly love to see them through the tough days ahead. Trey needed her moral support and Hannah could benefit from her experiences, as well as her female influence.

They needed her, whether they realized it or not. To be honest, she needed them just as much.

Determined to rush home then go straight over to his house, Sierra arrived at the nearest bus stop just as the bus was pulling away from the curb. She raced alongside for several feet and fortunately the driver recognized her.

"You almost missed me again, Dr. McAllaster," Rufus told her with a toothy smile as he welcomed her aboard.

"I know. Thanks for waiting."

Impatient at the bus's lumbering speed, Sierra counted the passing blocks and wondered if her budget would allow for a parking permit so she could avoid delays like this in the future. By the time she'd decided she could either drive or keep her internet service, she'd arrived.

In her hurry to get ready and go, she tossed her bag and her mail onto the table in her entryway and began shedding her clothes the minute she closed the front door. With one yank, she ripped open the snaps of her scrub top and headed down the hall to her bedroom.

"Well, now," came a lazy drawl from the living room. "This is an unexpected pleasure."

Sierra clutched the edges of her cotton shirt together. "Trey!" she exclaimed. "Mitch said you'd gone home to take a nap. I was changing so I could drive over and surprise you."

"Instead, I surprised you," he remarked. "I hope you don't mind, I made myself at home." His voice sounded odd.

"Not at all," she said. "That's why I showed you where I keep my spare key." She expected him to greet her with a kiss, but he didn't. While his eyes showed his appreciation for the view she'd unwillingly presented, he held himself stiffly, as if he was struggling for control.

As she studied him more closely, she realized he appeared just as haggard and drawn as Mitch had. She might not be a body-language expert, but his world had obviously tilted off its axis. For whatever reason, their meeting had driven him to despair, but she was glad of one fact.

He'd come to *her* for comfort.

A disappointed Trey watched Sierra refasten her shirt. He hadn't come here for an afternoon of delight, but the sight of her lacy blue bra made him want to haul her into her bedroom and bury himself deep inside her until he forgot everything, including his own name.

As tempting as the idea was, he couldn't use her as an anesthetic for his problems, no matter how badly the staff at his afternoon meeting had tried to chip away at his self-respect.

She studied him for a moment. "We both could use something to drink. Iced tea or a soda?"

"Do you have anything stronger?"

"Other than cooking sherry? No."

The decision seemed too difficult to make in his current state of mind. "Whatever you prefer is fine. Whatever is easiest."

She walked away. Unable to stand the separation because her presence was too calming, he followed her into the kitchen like a puppy dog begging for a treat. While she reached into the refrigerator, he sat at the table because a chair was handy and he was too emotionally spent to think about sitting anywhere else. As long as he was here, in the company of a woman who meant so much to him, he could handle himself.

She sat beside him and popped the soda tops. "Want to tell me what went wrong today?"

The concern in her voice shattered his composure. "What went wrong?" he bellowed loudly, harshly. "I'll tell you. *Everything.*"

Apparently unfazed by his outburst, she simply nodded. "Start at the beginning."

He drew a bracing breath and tried to organize his

thoughts. "The doctors in the unit decided against inserting a feeding tube for now. If Hannah doesn't gain one to three pounds this next week, they'll re-evaluate."

"A few pounds is a reasonable goal. I'll bet Hannah was happy about the feeding-tube situation."

"The prospect of being force-fed is definitely giving her an incentive to eat," he agreed.

"That's a positive step, wouldn't you agree?"

"Yes, but the worst is still to come," he said darkly. "As you probably know, Hannah will be treated by a team consisting of Lucy Quinn, a pediatrician—"

"I've met her and she's wonderful. I was hoping Hannah would be assigned to her."

He rubbed his face, hardly noticing the bristles he'd found. "Yeah, well, you got your wish."

If Sierra had noticed his sarcasm, she didn't comment.

"She also has Suzanne Hollister, a nutritionist, and Peggy Jones, a psychologist, on the team. They've told us that as soon as the worst of Hannah's health problems are resolved, and they should be in a few days, she'll move into an all-day outpatient program."

"Then Hannah will be able to go home every night. That's good news, too."

He nodded. "According to Peggy, dancers often suffer from anorexia because their weight is so critical to their careers. Because Hannah dances—as did her mother—she's predisposed to eating disorders."

"Then it's good you and her father will learn how to deal with her condition now. Did they mention how long she might be in therapy?"

"However long it takes," he said tiredly, "until they're satisfied Hannah is coping. According to them, anorexia is a form of post-traumatic stress disorder." He took a long swig of his soda.

"It is," she agreed. "A stressful event can affect one's self-image or create a sense of guilt that doesn't go away without an outlet. I presume you discussed the stressful events in her life—her mother's death, her father's drinking."

His laugh was humorless. "Here's where it turned nasty. I should have realized they had a plan when they separated Mitch and me. Dammit, I should have been prepared."

"Prepared for what?" she asked.

"Their questions." Unable to sit still, he jumped up and began to pace. "I shared what I knew, mentioning the subjects you did, but those two topics weren't enough for them. They kept pushing, pushing, pushing."

He met her gaze, unable to hide the pain he felt hours after the fact. The pain, and the humiliation, and the anger.

"They asked me… They asked me…" His voice caught in his throat and he didn't have the energy to force enough air through his vocal cords.

"They asked you what?" she coaxed.

He swallowed hard as he stood frozen in his tracks. "They asked if I knew about any physical or sexual abuse she may have suffered. Then they asked me if *I'd* abused my niece!" The urge to destroy something rose inside of him, just as it had during his meeting. At the time he would have liked nothing more than to drive his hand through the wall, but he'd possessed enough sense to know he'd only appear guilty. Sheer determination, along with his thoughts of running to Sierra when the grilling was over, had helped him cling to his temper and his sanity.

However, explaining this brought back every destructive urge full force. Without realizing what he was doing, he crumpled the can in his hand. "How could they ask me about those terrible things? I would *never* do anything to hurt her. I *love* her."

Sierra got up to wrap her arms around him. "You do. I'm sure they know it, too."

He snorted. "They had a funny way of showing it. They kept hammering at me, asking me if I'd done anything to her. Then they started asking if Mitch had abused her—if he had, would I deny it to protect him?" He snorted. "As if

I'd protect him from something so terrible. After everything we've been through, if I learn he ever so much as *thought* about doing such a thing..."

He rubbed the back of his neck, aware of how replaying this ugly scene made his chest hurt with every breath. "I should have intervened as soon as I suspected you might be right about her, but I didn't. Instead, I hoped things would get better, that we had time for Mitch to face up to his responsibilities and life would be good again."

"Don't be so hard on yourself," she said. "You gave him a deadline. Hannah's body simply escalated matters."

"I suppose, but I still can't believe the grilling they gave me. I'm a doctor, dedicated to healing people's pain. How could they think I'd abuse *anyone?*"

"Being a doctor doesn't automatically mean one is a good person, Trey."

"I know, but, dammit, Sierra, they made me feel dirty. Like a criminal. And I've known these people for years!"

"They hurt your pride," she agreed, "which is always more painful than we'd expect. It's devastating to be accused of horrible acts when you know they aren't true."

He drew a deep breath. "They ran Mitch through the same gauntlet. I was lucky, though. I could leave—and I did—but he had to stay with Hannah and pretend as if no one believed we were monsters."

"They had to ask, Trey," she said softly. "Forty to sixty percent of people with anorexia have been abused in one form or another. They have to discover the truth before the healing process can begin."

"Well, they were wrong. I didn't do anything and neither did Mitch."

"Now they know and can hunt for another stressor that set off her habits," she said kindly. "It's similar to what we do in medicine, Trey. We always look for the most common cause of people's symptoms. After we rule out the obvious, we dig deeper. They've ruled out abuse and now they'll look in another direction."

He rested his chin on the top of her head, emotionally spent but feeling more in control now that he'd spewed out his poisonous anger. "What happened with your sister?"

"Date rape," she answered. "None of us knew until the clinic staff ferreted out the problem. Once the secret of that night was out in the open, she could move on with her life in a healthier way."

Secrets. Everything came down to secrets. Oh, how he hated them.

"That's part of the problem," he admitted. "I'm afraid of what they might find. What if someone we've known and trusted has taken liberties? A teacher, a friend's parent, a—"

She placed her fingers against his mouth. "I suspect the truth won't be as bad as you suspect."

"What makes you say that?"

"I talked to Hannah before I came home tonight. Mind you, I'm not a therapist and my expertise in this area is limited, but I think Hannah is trying to become a miniature version of her mother."

"What? Why?"

"She's smart enough to compare a before-and-after picture of her father. She believes he doesn't love her."

"He does!"

"I'm sure he does. However, if one looks at this from Hannah's perspective, it's easy to see why she'd question his amount of affection. He was happy before her mother died and now he isn't. He came home every night and now he doesn't. In essence, he was there for her mother, but not for her.

"She wanted her dad back, Trey, and if becoming the dancer Marcy was would make her dad happy again and cause him to love her, she was willing to do whatever was necessary."

"It seems so simple. So obvious."

"I'm sure there are other factors, too, but this gives Lucy

and Peggy a starting point." She rested her cheek against his chest. "Relax. You're off the hook."

"No, I'm not. I should have seen the signs," he insisted.

"You did the best you could."

He shook his head. "I didn't. I failed her and I failed Marcy."

"How?"

He hadn't realized it would be so difficult to put his feelings into words. "When the oncologist gave Marcy a few days to live at best, in one of her rare, lucid moments she called me into her room and asked me to look after her daughter. She was afraid Mitch wouldn't adjust well to her death."

"You've mentioned he'd been in denial, so it's understandable she'd want a backup. You were her brother-in-law, so who else could she ask?"

"No one. She had a sister, but Marcy was a change-of-life baby and the two weren't close. The thing is, she wasn't asking me as a brother-in-law. She was asking me as friends who had a long history. In fact, there was a time we were inseparable."

Sierra tried to understand this new aspect of his family dynamics with an open mind, but she couldn't. Obviously, her thoughts must have been written on her face because he started to laugh.

"I hope you never play poker except with me," he teased, "because I can tell what you're thinking. In this case, you'd be wrong. Our relationship was strictly platonic. Marcy and I met in college when we'd both registered for a jazz dancing class. Have you ever met someone who made you feel as if you'd known them forever, and you'd only met them? That's how it was for Marcy and me. She was magic in motion and I had two left feet, so we spent a lot of hours practicing our dance steps. We spent every free moment during that semester together because she was determined to turn me into the next Fred Astaire." He paused with a grin. "Trust me, she failed."

Sierra fought her blush, hating that she'd jumped to

the wrong conclusion. "Then how did she marry your brother?"

"I organized a blind date. I sensed the two of them had a lot in common, and I was right." He eyed her carefully. "You thought I was having an affair with her, didn't you?"

"Only for a moment because it was entirely possible," she defended. "Relationships can be complicated. For all I knew, *you* could be Hannah's father."

"I could be," he agreed, "if Marcy and I hadn't realized from the beginning that we were content to be friends."

"How did you feel when she and your brother had a special connection that didn't include you?"

"I was happy for them," he answered simply. "They were two people who, when you saw them together, were meant to be a couple. I couldn't have been happier when Hannah was born and I became a doting uncle."

He sighed. "Which is why I get so frustrated with him. He wasn't the only one who lost someone special. For us, though, life went on. Mitch remained stuck in pity-party mode."

"It's a comfortable place to be," she agreed. "You can drift along without expectations, either from yourself or other people. You have to fight to move forward and it's certainly easier not to, especially when family and friends pick up the slack."

He grew thoughtful. "I've filled the gap for longer than I should have," he admitted, "but if I hadn't, he would have sent Hannah away. Marcy had been against that option and she wanted me to do everything I could so it wouldn't happen. In the end, though, Hannah still suffered."

"Her collapse is *not* your fault."

He sighed. "I want to believe it, but it's hard."

"As her uncle," Sierra began slowly, "your options were limited. If she hadn't ended up in Emergency, you would have cornered Mitch on Friday, like you'd planned. Given how you're a master of persuasion, you would have convinced him to take appropriate measures."

The guilt in his eyes eased, which suggested that she was getting through to him.

"I realize you came close to losing her, but maybe Mitch will listen and pay closer attention to his daughter now. This was his wake-up call, too. He now knows how badly Hannah wants her dad back."

He pulled her back in his embrace with a heartfelt sigh. "I knew I needed to come here."

"I'm glad you did," she answered. "Feeling better?"

"Much better. I still could use some TLC, though. It's been a trying day and I missed being with you." He ran his finger just above her neckline and a question appeared in his eyes.

"How much time do you have? I presume you want to go back to the hospital and spell your brother?"

"I thought I'd drop by after dinner. We'd have a couple of hours."

She smiled at him before she grabbed his hand and led him out of the kitchen. "Good, because I know exactly how to pass the time."

For the next week, whenever Trey spent the evening at the hospital with Hannah, Sierra accompanied him. She always brought some sort of card game to play and he was becoming quite expert at gin rummy, spoons and, Hannah's favorite, old maid. Sierra would stay until visiting hours ended, while he spent the night with Hannah on the daybed provided for family members.

On the day of Hannah's discharge, Trey and Sierra planned a welcome-home party for her, complete with ice cream and cake.

"She probably won't eat more than a bite or two," Sierra cautioned.

"That's okay. If she eats some of it, I'll be happy."

Later, after they'd eaten the cake before lunch because as Sierra told her, "Life is short so eat dessert first," Trey pulled Mitch aside.

"How are you doing?" he asked.

Mitch shrugged. "I'm okay."

"Are you sure?" Trey didn't think Mitch looked quite right, but perhaps it was because he was scared stiff about dealing with Hannah's eating disorder. "You know you can call me anytime."

"I know, but we'll be okay. The team told me what to watch for, so I'll keep an eagle eye on her."

"Okay."

Mitch exhaled. "You've been telling me this for years, so you'll be pleased to hear I've also taken a leave of absence from my job. My district manager is trying to find a spot for me closer to home and with limited, if any, travel. The psychologist told me how Hannah is struggling because I'm away so much, so I'm going to try to be here for her."

"Hannah needs you like she needs no one else." As Trey said the words, he knew them to be true. As much as he loved Hannah, she wasn't his to love as anything more than his niece.

"Thanks. Now, why don't you take your lady home?" Mitch said, eyeing Sierra and Hannah as they giggled over something. "My daughter and I need some one-on-one time and if I'm not mistaken, you have your own relationship to work on."

The concept of building a relationship with Sierra caught him off guard. He hadn't set out to include her in his life, but circumstances had put her there. In fact, it became difficult to imagine going back to his pre-Sierra days when his life had been merely a string of short-term flings. She had taught him that letting someone close, allowing them to share his burden, didn't have to be a painful experience.

He liked to think that he'd helped her, too. Although she hadn't mentioned her future career plans, he sensed she was much more relaxed these days. Traumas didn't cause her to become tense, like they once had.

In essence, they'd helped each other overcome their fears. What more could he ask from anyone?

Over the next week, Trey concentrated on Sierra as he mentally planned their future. Sierra had prepared dinner for the four of them one night and Hannah had done considerable justice to her meal.

The evening reminded Trey of the days when Marcy had been presiding over their table. She would have approved of Sierra, he was certain.

The idea of making her an official part of the family began to take hold. Unfortunately, his life—which had settled into a pleasant routine—changed a few days later.

"Uncle Trey?" Hannah's shaky voice came over the phone on Thursday morning.

Instantly, he was awake. "Yeah, hon. What's wrong?"

"Something's wrong with Daddy. He doesn't know who I am or where he is. Uncle Trey? I'm scared."

"Don't worry, sweetheart," he said calmly, although he was worried enough for both of them. "I'm on my way. And don't be frightened if an ambulance gets there before I do. Let the paramedics inside, okay?"

Trey dialed 911 as he dived into a pair of athletic shorts and a T-shirt. After reporting the situation to the dispatcher, he texted Sierra at the hospital to warn her of Mitch's arrival. Seconds later, he hopped into his car and tore into the street with his tires squealing in his rush to get to Mitch's house. Part of him wanted to be at the hospital, but there would be plenty of people on hand to lend medical assistance. Hannah, on the other hand, would need someone and he was all she had left.

CHAPTER TEN

SIERRA eyed the text message and her heart sank. Hadn't Trey's family gone through enough the past few weeks? She warned the nurses on duty moments before another text message came through.

Thirty-six-year-old male, delirious. ETA three minutes.

Sierra immediately ran through a mental list of causes for delirium. An acute illness, perhaps, or a side effect of medication. Had his doctor, or Trey for that matter, prescribed a drug to help him deal with Hannah's condition—a drug his body had rejected?

Speculation ceased as the ambulance arrived.

"He doesn't know where he is and if not for his daughter, we wouldn't know his name," a paramedic told her. "Vital signs are unremarkable."

"Mitch, do you know where you are?" she asked, noting IV fluid was running steadily into his vein.

"No. Where am I? What am I doing here?" He raised his arm to gaze at the tubing taped to his hand. "What's this for?"

His confusion wasn't a good indicator, she thought as she ordered blood and urine tests in her hope to discover the cause. Her opinion didn't change when, other than a mild fever and a slightly rapid heartbeat, she didn't find anything to account for his delirium.

Trey hadn't arrived yet, but he would and he would demand answers she couldn't provide. She ordered more tests—an

EKG, a chest X-ray and a CT scan—to rule out a heart attack, stroke or a tumor.

Trey finally strode into the trauma room. "What have we got?" he asked grimly.

Sierra pulled him away from the bed. "Not much. Your brother is extremely confused and disoriented. I've ordered tests to check for an infection, a heart attack and a stroke."

"And?" he demanded.

"We're still waiting." She glanced into the hallway. "Where's Hannah?"

"She's in the staff lounge." He held up his hands. "I know what you're thinking—she shouldn't be left alone right now, and you'd be right. I'll sit with her until it's time for her therapy session, but I wanted to see for myself what was going on rather than wait for an update."

Mitch moved restlessly on the bed as he mumbled gibberish.

"Another possibility is a drug side-effect," Sierra said carefully. "Is he taking any meds, or had one recently prescribed?"

"Not that I'm aware of. He's always been remarkably healthy and never liked to take anything stronger than ibuprofen."

"You said he's a pharmaceutical salesman. This is a long shot, but he has access to samples. Would he self-medicate?"

"No." His answer was quick, his expression dark. "He wouldn't."

Considering the man had been addicted to alcohol, it wouldn't take much to progress to abusing prescription drugs. "Are you certain? Beyond all doubt?"

He opened his mouth to argue, but the fighting light in his eyes faded. "No, I'm not."

Sierra made a mental note to request a toxicology screen. "Did he eat or drink anything unusual?"

"Hannah said no. She fixed grilled cheese sandwiches and lemonade last night with her usual brownies for dessert. He normally drinks his morning coffee about the time she gets up, and when he wasn't downstairs, she found him in bed, confused. She called me and I called EMS."

Sierra sighed. "Not a lot to go on," she remarked. "Maybe the tests will show us the answers."

Unfortunately, they didn't. The EKG and CT scans were normal and he wasn't dehydrated or anemic. His white count fell within acceptable range and his urine tests were negative for infection. So were his tox screens.

"No joy with the lab results," she told him a few hours later. "Our next option is a spinal tap."

"Do what you have to do," he said tiredly.

Her pager went off again and this time the message was blunt.

Trauma One. Stat.

"It's Mitch," she said, grateful that Hannah was currently engrossed in a television program. "Gotta go."

Inside, the nurse greeted her at the trauma-room doorway. "He just pulled out his IV. His temp spiked to 102 and he's extremely agitated and hallucinating. He needs restraints."

"Okay." Sierra knew it would be rough on Trey to see his brother tied down, but what could they do?

"Would benzos work?" Roma asked.

From over her shoulder, Trey answered for her. "A benzodiazepine could make delirium symptoms worse. I'd suggest an antipsychotic instead."

Roma glanced at Sierra for confirmation and she gave it with a nod.

"Let's hope he won't go into cardiac arrest or have a stroke before the medicine takes effect," he said.

She placed a hand on his arm. "I know this isn't easy on you. Take Hannah for a soda and a cookie. I'll text you if there's a change."

"All right." But in spite of his plan to leave, Trey simply couldn't. He stood beside Mitch's bed and mentally ran through his symptoms, trying to correlate them with his medical history. The idea that popped into his head wasn't one he liked, but it offered the only logical explanation.

"Roma," he said. "Cancel that last order. Give him benzo instead."

Roma froze. "Dr. McAllaster said—"

"Just do it." He turned to Sierra. "He's in DTs."

"Delirium tremens?" she echoed. "I thought he quit drinking years ago."

"Obviously not," he said grimly. "And if he *has* been drinking, he probably stopped cold turkey after Hannah landed in the hospital. Regardless of the details, my diagnosis is correct. It's the only explanation." He turned to Roma. "In a nutshell, benzos function like alcohol on certain receptors and will induce a sedated state. Then, as his body adjusts, we can taper off the drugs while his brain resets itself."

"If you're wrong," Sierra warned, "you'll only make the situation worse."

"Unfortunately, I'm not. Wait and see."

Roma injected the medication into Mitch's IV port and shortly after, as if on cue, Mitch relaxed into a near-normal sleep.

Trey felt his own strain. His shoulders slumped as he gazed down at his brother. As a physician, he would have prided himself on his correct diagnosis, but now his success only filled him with sadness, disappointment and anger. At one time, he and Mitch had confided in each other and shared opinions with lively discussions, but obviously Mitch now considered him to be so unapproachable that he'd chosen to drink in secret rather than let Trey help him.

As Trey took a hard look at the big picture of his life, he regretted missing the signs that hindsight showed him and worried about what it meant for the future. How could he ever give a woman the emotional support and stability she deserved when he'd plainly fallen short with his own brother and niece?

Lost in his thoughts, he didn't protest when Sierra hauled

him into the physicians' office where she poured him a bracing cup of coffee.

Trey leaned weakly against the desk, still reeling from this latest personal disaster. "What am I going to tell Hannah?"

He'd posed his question to himself, but Sierra answered. "The truth," she said simply.

"This will set her progress back."

"It might, but give her treatment team some credit. They'll help you see her through this. Now, drink your coffee and then reassure your niece that her dad will be okay."

For the next three days, Sierra noticed Trey become less talkative and more preoccupied. His mood was understandable, given his family circumstances, but what hurt her most was how he seemed to distance himself from her. He didn't encourage spending their evenings together and whenever she suggested an outing that included Hannah, he countered with a ready excuse.

She tried to make allowances—to believe he was simply overwhelmed with Mitch's drinking on top of Hannah's problems—but his remoteness wasn't easy to accept. She wanted him to lean on her, to share his thoughts and feelings, but he wouldn't. The same sense of powerlessness she'd felt with David crept up on her. Now, like then, she didn't know what to do to change the situation.

The caseload in Emergency had slowed that afternoon so while everyone milled around the nurses' station to offer their theories for their unexpected slow spell and Trey had slipped away to visit his brother, she strolled outside for a breath of fresh air.

Out of habit, she began walking the labyrinth, but by the time she'd progressed halfway, Hannah was barreling toward her, ponytail flying, tears flowing.

She caught her. "What's wrong, Hannah?"

Hannah sniffled, then gulped, then sniffled again. "It's Daddy," she hiccuped.

Immediate fear struck Sierra. "What's wrong?"

Hannah shook her head as she shuddered. "Everything," she wailed as if her heart was broken. "He's...he's going to send me away!"

"Send you away?" Sierra couldn't believe it. "Are you sure?"

Hannah's head bobbed and more tears flowed. "I heard him tell...Uncle Trey...just now. I don't want to go-o-o-o." She fell into Sierra's embrace and wept until her tears soaked through Sierra's scrub top.

"Oh, honey. I'm sure there's been a mistake," Sierra crooned, unable to believe Mitch would act so rashly. There had to be a logical explanation. "Maybe you misunderstood."

"I did all this for nothing," Hannah moaned.

Sierra's instincts went on alert. "What did you do for nothing?" she repeated.

The child hiccuped a few more times as she tried to explain. "I tried to do everything...to not be a bother...so he wouldn't ever send me away, but he's doing it...*anyway!*"

"Your dad is sending you away?" Sierra repeated.

Hannah nodded. "When Daddy was sick the last time," she said dully, "I heard him and Uncle Trey talk about sending me to Aunt Sylvia's. Daddy said he'd wait and see how things worked out. I tried so hard to show him how much he *needed* me. I was good at it, too, because everybody was happy. Then I got sick."

Sierra brushed the strands of loose hair off Hannah's damp face. "It isn't your job to make the situation easy or to take on your dad's responsibility," she said kindly.

Hannah clearly wasn't listening. "And now Daddy thinks I'm a bother 'cause I've been in the hospital and we need counseling and—"

"Your dad is only trying to do what he thinks is best for you, so you can get better," she said, hoping she was right. Hoping that Mitch wasn't rejecting Hannah.

"But I don't want to *go* to Utah," the youngster began to wail again. "My friends are here. Uncle Trey, *everybody!*"

"I'll talk to your dad," Sierra said, determined to get to the bottom of this. She glanced up to see Trey striding forward and never felt happier to see him than in that moment.

"Thank goodness you're here," she told him. "What is going on?"

Dreading what had to come next, he crouched beside them to pull Hannah out of Sierra's embrace. "Honey, wait inside for a minute while I talk to Sierra."

"Don't let him send me away, Uncle Trey," she begged. "Please? Tell him I'll do *anything* he wants me to."

"I will," he promised. "Now, don't worry, okay?"

"But—"

"Don't worry," he repeated.

She swiped her nose with one hand then nodded. "Okay."

Sierra waited to ask the obvious until the two of them were alone. "What's all this about?" she asked.

He exhaled slowly, his face grim. "He's gotten this idea that he's too dependent on me and it's interfering with my life and our relationship."

"But…that's not true," she protested. "Hannah isn't interfering and neither is anything or anyone else."

"Yeah, well, Mitch thinks it would be in everyone's best interests if he sent Hannah to live with her aunt for a while."

Sierra was stunned. "I hope you told him he was wrong."

"I did, but he wouldn't listen." He raked his hair with his fingers. "Do you know how long it took to convince him not to call Marcy's sister then and there? To persuade him to sleep on his decision? To beg him to run this by Hannah's treatment team before he bought a plane ticket?"

"Oh, Trey. What can we do? We can't let him send her away. She'll see it as a rejection and will be crushed."

"I know. I'll do whatever it takes to stop him."

Between his grim tone and the way he avoided her gaze, a shiver of fear ran down Sierra's spine. "What do you have in mind?" she asked.

He seemed reluctant to speak, which set off more alarms.

"You can't deny we *have* spent a lot of time together. I might have headed off a lot of these problems if I'd—"

"You're saying I'm at fault?" A roaring noise sounded in her ears, reminding her of how David's family had heaped blame on her. Their vitriol hadn't bothered her nearly as much as Trey's accusation because Trey's family had felt like her own. She'd even begun to treat them as if they were...

"No, I'm saying if I'd concentrated on them instead—"

Knowing Trey's do-it-himself attitude, the point of his roundabout conversation was obvious. And painful. "You want us to go our separate ways."

"Only for a while. Until I can sort out everything and get Mitch and Hannah back on the road to recovery."

She couldn't believe he was so blind. "I hate to disappoint you, Trey, but you'll never sort out everything. Every day brings a new problem and a new challenge. The best way to survive them is to stand together and lean on each other. We can show Mitch our hearts are big enough to include Hannah and anyone else who needs us. Give us a chance," she begged.

"Look at how I struggled to keep things afloat before Hannah collapsed. It won't be easier now."

"But I'll be with you," she pointed out. "I can help you help them. Please let me."

"I'm sorry," he said, stony-faced. "I wish it could be otherwise."

Her legs suddenly seemed too weak to hold her. She stared at him, hardly able to see through the tears shimmering in her eyes.

"No, you don't," she said quietly, understanding why he'd been so preoccupied lately. "I honestly believed you were different, but you aren't. You're nothing but a coward, Trey Donovan. We could make this work if you wanted to, but I suspect you've been waiting for an excuse to end things. Mitch simply handed one to you."

She tossed her head as she squared her shoulders. "You're

a fool for throwing away a beautiful relationship, which I can assure you doesn't come around all that often. But do you know who's the bigger fool? I am, because I loved you far more deeply than I ever loved my own husband. And, like him, you didn't appreciate it and definitely don't deserve it."

Trey walked back to Mitch's room, his footsteps as heavy as his spirits. Learning Sierra loved him should have been a happy event, and instead the news was bittersweet.

You've been waiting for an excuse to end things. Mitch simply handed one to you.

He'd thought about making her a permanent addition to his family, but had he simply gotten cold feet?

No, this had nothing to do with losing his nerve. Mitch had simply reminded him of where his priorities belonged.

Then why did he feel so awful? Why did it seem as if all the light had suddenly disappeared, leaving him in total darkness?

He strode into Mitch's room a few minutes later.

"What happened to you?" Mitch demanded. "You look like hell."

Trey certainly felt as if he was there, but this was the path he'd chosen. "You were right. A romance with Sierra would be too difficult to juggle, with everything going on in our family."

Mitch's tension visibly eased. "I'm glad you're finally seeing this from my point of view."

"Yeah, that's why I broke up with Sierra."

"You…" Mitch turned bug-eyed. "You what?"

Trey nodded. "Under the circumstances, I had to. I know how much of a sacrifice you'd be making to send Hannah away, so now you don't have to. We'll continue just as we did before." The thought wasn't as satisfying as he'd hoped it would be.

"You broke up with Sierra?" Mitch repeated.

"It seemed like the best option."

"But…but you weren't supposed to do that," Mitch protested. "You two belong together."

"Maybe, maybe not. If we're meant to be, she'll still be around after Hannah's back on the straight and narrow. "Now," he said firmly in a brisk, I'm-changing-the-subject tone, "we should organize our schedules. I'd hate Hannah to miss any appointments with her therapist."

Mitch shook his head. "I can't let you throw away your life for us. I won't let you. Besides, Hannah needs a mother's influence. She'll be better off with Sylvia."

You've been waiting for an excuse…

Sierra had suggested Mitch had given one to him. But what if…what if Trey and Sierra herself had given one to Mitch? It would certainly explain a lot. If his theory was correct, he'd made a colossal mistake.

The idea made his blood run cold.

"Now that I think about it," he said slowly, so his racing thoughts could catch up, "sending Hannah to a stranger won't benefit anyone but you."

"Me?" Mitch avoided his gaze. "How?"

"I'm surprised I didn't see this before," he said in wonderment. "You've wanted Hannah out of your life for the last few years, but I always talked you into keeping her. You've been *waiting for an excuse,* haven't you?" As he used Sierra's own words, he hated that he'd hurt the one woman who'd been willing to stand beside him without asking anything in return.

"I only want what's best—"

"For you," Trey finished for him. "I overheard part of what Hannah told Sierra downstairs. She heard us talking the last time you wanted to send her to Sylvia's and she's been afraid of that happening ever since. Did you ever wonder why or even *notice* how she does everything possible to be helpful? She didn't want you to consider her a nuisance and send her away."

"I never thought she was a nuisance," Mitch defended.

"It doesn't matter what you think. It's what *Hannah* thinks. Her logic explains why she became the perfect child, the perfect imitation of Marcy. In her mind, if you depended on her, you'd always need her, so she made certain she took on everything from preparing dinner to doing laundry and taking out the trash. As far as she's concerned, her efforts weren't enough to suit you. I'll bet you a steak dinner that her eating problems began that day.

"What I really find disgusting," he added coldly, "is how you hid behind me—used *me*—for your dirty work while you seemed so caring. If you can't be her father, at least be honest and tell her the truth. Don't sell your stupid idea under the guise of doing me a favor. She'll resent me as much as she'll resent you. Unless, of course, that's your whole plan."

The pieces fell into place. "That's it," Trey said slowly. "You're jealous of my relationship with your daughter."

"No."

"I'm right and we both know it."

"Okay," Mitch grumbled. "It bugs me when I know you do a better job at parenting than I do."

"You're her father," Trey reminded him. "Not me. She knows that. Why do you think she calls you every night when you're on the road? I support and encourage her as much as I can, but I can't take your place."

"You shouldn't have to raise my daughter," Mitch muttered.

"Oh, so I can't help you, but a woman who's only seen Hannah a handful of times during the last five years *can?*" Trey shook his head. "Where's the rationale behind that?"

Mitch didn't answer.

"If you don't want me to raise your daughter, don't ask me to," he said bluntly. "I've suggested this before and I'll say it again. Find a job that doesn't involve traveling if your current boss can't work out something. Come home every night. If it's too difficult being in the same house you shared with Marcy, buy a different one. Be proactive and get on with your life."

"Aren't you going to tell me what you *really* think?" Mitch asked wryly.

"The really sad thing is how I've trodden lightly on this subject for far too long because I was afraid of what you might do. Well, no more. If you can't be the father she needs, give me custody. Don't ship her away like a piece of unwanted clothing."

Mitch fell silent. "I know my actions don't prove it, but I really do want her. She's all I have left of Marcy. It's just that I've made such a mess of things. I couldn't even stop drinking without causing a disaster," he said, sounding disgusted. "If I screw up again—"

The comment reminded Trey of how he'd made his own mistakes with Sierra. He should have listened to her, trusted her, but instead he'd destroyed the one thing he cherished. Mitch's little incident hadn't set his priorities in order, as he'd first thought. It had turned them upside down.

Trey's fund of compassion for his brother was suddenly overdrawn. "Then grow a spine so you can make damn sure you get it right."

Mitch grew quiet. "Did you and Sierra really break up, or was this all an act?"

Trey rubbed his eyes tiredly. The hurt he'd seen in her eyes—the hurt he'd put there—would haunt him for a long time. For a man who supposedly always knew the right things to say, he'd completely missed the mark. "It wasn't an act," he answered flatly, although he wished it had been. Now he had to undo the damage.

Mitch gave a disgusted snort. "And you think *I've* done stupid things during my life? Still, I wouldn't lose too much sleep over it. Turn on your famous charm and she'll be putty in your hands."

Trey disagreed. Sierra was the one woman who wouldn't fall for flattering words and a big smile.

* * *

"Dr. McAllaster? Dr. McAllaster?"

Sierra broke herself out of her daze to see Roma standing in the doorway of the physicians' office. "Yes?" she asked.

The woman appeared uncomfortable, and somewhat worried. "Dr. Keegan's looking for you."

"Send him in."

Roma didn't move. She simply peered at her. "Are you okay?"

She didn't think she'd ever be okay again. No, she would, because she'd experienced worse things and lived to tell the tale, but it wouldn't be easy. She simply needed time to recover from the crushing blow of Trey's rejection.

"Yeah, sure. I'm fine."

The nurse didn't seem convinced, but she simply nodded. "I'll tell him you're here."

A few minutes later, Lane Keegan appeared in the doorway. "Sierra," he said jovially. "How's life in Emergency?"

"Just fine," she said, forcing enthusiasm into her voice.

"Great, great. I wanted to let you know we have two very promising candidates for this position. Either of them would be able to start within a few weeks. How does that sound?"

"Wonderful." Under the circumstances, she was supremely grateful to be leaving Emergency far sooner than her originally planned sixty days.

"I've heard good things about your work down here," he said. "I know I'd promised you could return to fifth floor medical, but if you'd rather remain in this department, the choice is yours. I only need to know before we offer your spot to one of our candidates."

She thought a moment. Thanks to Trey, her stint in Emergency had served its purpose. She'd rediscovered her joy and the fulfillment she'd once enjoyed. If the situation with Trey hadn't turned out so badly, she would have been willing to stay. At the moment, though, she simply didn't want to work where she'd encounter him regularly.

Her other option was to cover another shift so their paths

wouldn't cross, but that scenario wouldn't necessarily be any better. Seeing his scrawl at the bottom of a memo tacked to the bulletin board, finding his coffee-stained mug in the lounge and catching a whiff of his particular brand of after-shave as she walked past his locker would be reminders she didn't need. Absence, she'd decided, was the perfect prescription to recover from a lost love.

"Thank you, but I'd like to return to the fifth floor."

He nodded. "Fair enough. I'll let you know when we have a date in mind."

Tomorrow wouldn't be soon enough.

Sierra gathered her purse from her locker and headed out the door. She started toward her bus stop then changed her mind. She couldn't go home yet. Trey's presence was too fresh there for her to find any peace. She needed to burn off her frustration and energy first, and the only place she could was in the labyrinth.

Outside, she stowed her bag under a bench and began walking the circles. Trey's decision to live his life without her was his loss, not hers. The news had been painful, but she'd survive like she'd survived all her other disappointments, she told herself as she turned left, then right, then left, then right. The back-and-forth motion was supposed to give the peaceful sensation of rocking in a cradle, but she wasn't feeling it.

She wouldn't leave until she did, she decided. No matter how many times she had to walk this path, or how late she remained, she'd travel it until she found her inner peace and Trey's rejection no longer felt as if he'd torn out her heart.

Trey watched Sierra as she walked the labyrinth. Actually, she was practically running down the paths, which suggested how upset she was. He'd been such a jerk and now he had to undo the damage. At least she was outdoors and had nothing handy to throw at him, although, as Hannah had informed him, he deserved it.

After ten minutes of bolstering his courage, ten minutes

of watching for her steps to slow, ten minutes of practicing his speech, he hoped for the best as he made his move.

Sierra's feet began to ache, making her realize she'd walked at a much faster clip than she should have for maximum benefit of the labyrinth exercise. She honestly couldn't say if her walk had helped her find inner peace, but she was definitely tired, so it hadn't been a wasted experience.

Without warning, someone fell into step beside her. Hoping it wasn't someone who wanted a neighborly chat, she glanced up and discovered it was Trey.

Her breath froze in her chest.

He looked wonderful—so tall and handsome.

He looked awful—his smile was missing and his eyes held uncertainty.

"If you're looking for Hannah, she isn't here," she stated flatly.

"I was looking for you."

"Why?"

He paused. "Did you ever do something you thought was right, but it turned into your worst mistake?"

Loving you, she silently answered.

"You talked about waiting for excuses. When I spoke with Mitch, I realized he'd been waiting for one, too. You and I gave it to him. And foolishly I used his decision as a reminder that I was better off handling problems on my own. That I didn't have room for anyone else."

She stopped abruptly and held up her hands. "Don't tell me you've suddenly discovered the error of your ways in a few short hours. I won't believe you cast off your lifelong views so quickly. It's impossible."

"Since I met you, I've had to constantly revise those views. Unfortunately, Mitch's incident made me forget the lessons I'd learned. The lessons you'd taught me—that sharing problems made them bearable. I need you beside me, poking me, prodding me, supporting me, loving me as much as I love you."

Sierra brushed at a loose lock of hair with a shaky hand.

He'd said the right words in the right tone, but she'd been fooled before by a man who spoke eloquently. She didn't trust her instincts anymore.

Not knowing what to say, she simply kept walking.

He planted himself in front of her. "I know you aren't sure I'm being honest and truthful, and I don't blame you, but remember the day of the gunshot trauma? You said you hadn't passed your test with flying colors but you wanted to take the exam again. I flunked my test, but I can pass it the next time. I promise."

Her hurt demanded that she deny him the opportunity to redeem himself, but his argument made it impossible. He'd given her a second chance. Couldn't she do the same?

As if he sensed her resolve was wavering, he threaded her arm through his and began walking. "I want to stroll along the labyrinth of our life as a couple, helping each other navigate the twists and turns we'll encounter. Maybe we'll have financial problems or maybe one of us will have an illness. Mitch and Hannah—"

"What about them?" she demanded. "Is he sending her to—?"

"She's staying right here. I can also assure you that the question won't come up again."

"I'm glad."

"They might require extra attention from us for a while, and our kids will probably give us both gray hair—"

"Aren't you jumping ahead of yourself by talking about children?" she asked.

"I'm *looking* ahead," he corrected. "The point is, no matter what comes, no matter *who* appears in our life, we'll face those situations together, not separately."

The promises he gave created a lump of longing in her throat. She squeezed her eyes shut because she didn't want the tears she'd been holding back to run down her face.

"In the weeks we've known each other, we've balanced our areas of weakness," he added. "You taught me how to share my personal burdens and I like to think I helped you regain your professional confidence. We both did something for each other that no one else could. That has to mean something."

"It does, but will it be strong enough to survive the next catastrophe?" she asked.

"There will be times when I'll do something stupid or unintentional. You'll forgive me because you have a forgiving heart and because of one undeniable truth. You'll know you're the center of my life, Sierra. You, and no one else."

She'd told herself not to be charmed by his words, but how could she resist? "Oh, Trey."

He grabbed both her hands. "We're getting married, Sierra. Next week, next year, or whenever you're ready, but it will happen because I don't want to imagine my life without you. I *can't* imagine it without you."

"What about Hannah and Mitch?"

"Mitch was horrified when I told him what I'd done. As for Hannah, I think you know how she'd react."

"You're really proposing."

"I am. So say yes, because we're meant for each other. Say yes, because you're my better half. Say yes, because I love you."

She smiled at that. "Yes."

His eyes filled with tenderness and as he kissed her, Sierra heard one word in the distance—a word uttered by a young female voice.

"Yippee!"

Medical Romance™

FLIRTING WITH THE SOCIETY DOCTOR
by Janice Lynn

Faith Fogarty has spent *months* fighting her attraction to spectacular doctor Vale Wakefield, but now, facing a weekend as Vale's date—to a society wedding!—it's time Faith took a few risks with the delicious doctor…

WHEN ONE NIGHT ISN'T ENOUGH
by Wendy S Marcus

Nurse Ali Forshay is horrified when she realises that she's crazily in lust with Dr Jared Padget—the man she loves to hate! The conclusion: spend a feverish night together! It would be a strictly one-time-only experience… Wouldn't it?

MELTING THE ARGENTINE DOCTOR'S HEART
by Meredith Webber

Scarred in an accident, Dr Jorge Suárez turns his back on everything except his work. Until his beautiful ex, Caroline, arrives, with their adorable daughter who calls him 'Papa'. Dr Jorge is starting to feel again—whether he wants to or not…

SMALL TOWN MARRIAGE MIRACLE
by Jennifer Taylor

Returning to Avondale was supposed to bring a well-earned rest for surgeon Emma Roberts—not a confrontation with Dr Daniel Kennedy, who broke her heart! Emma isn't about to forgive him in a hurry—unless Avondale can work its magic…

**On sale from 3rd June 2011
Don't miss out!**

Available at WHSmith, Tesco, ASDA, Eason and all good bookshops
www.millsandboon.co.uk

Medical Romance™

ST PIRAN'S: PRINCE ON THE CHILDREN'S WARD
by Sarah Morgan

Children's doctor Tasha O'Hara's new job is looking after a sinfully gorgeous, injured Mediterranean prince. This isn't just *any* prince, but heartbreaker Prince Alessandro Cavalieri. Alessandro's definition of No Physical Activity *definitely* goes against doctor's orders…and it's becoming impossible for Tasha not to succumb to temptation!

HARRY ST CLAIR: ROGUE OR DOCTOR?
by Fiona McArthur

Harry St Clair does a good job persuading people that the devil-may-care rogue is the real him, but midwife Bonnie McKenzie isn't fooled! The real Harry St Clair is one of the best doctors in the southern hemisphere. The real Harry St Clair is buried under the weight of his devastating secrets—a weight he no longer has to carry alone…

**On sale from 3rd June 2011
Don't miss out!**

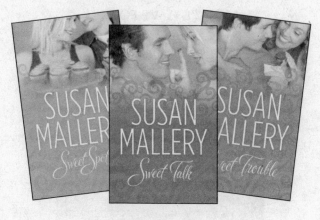

2 FREE BOOKS
AND A SURPRISE GIFT

We would like to take this opportunity to thank you for reading this Mills & Boon® book by offering you the chance to take TWO more specially selected books from the Medical™ series absolutely FREE! We're also making this offer to introduce you to the benefits of the Mills & Boon® Book Club™—

- **FREE home delivery**
- **FREE gifts and competitions**
- **FREE monthly Newsletter**
- **Exclusive Mills & Boon Book Club offers**
- **Books available before they're in the shops**

Accepting these FREE books and gift places you under no obligation to buy, you may cancel at any time, even after receiving your free books. Simply complete your details below and return the entire page to the address below. You don't even need a stamp!

YES Please send me 2 free Medical books and a surprise gift. I understand that unless you hear from me, I will receive 5 superb new stories every month including two 2-in-1 books priced at £5.30 each and a single book priced at £3.30, postage and packing free. I am under no obligation to purchase any books and may cancel my subscription at any time. The free books and gift will be mine to keep in any case.

Ms/Mrs/Miss/Mr _____ Initials _____

Surname _____

Address _____

_____

_____ Postcode _____

E-mail _____

Send this whole page to: Mills & Boon Book Club, Free Book Offer, FREEPOST NAT 10298, Richmond, TW9 1BR